Just Another Zombie Love Story:

Chivalry is Undead

M. A. Rogers

Cover art and design by Cathy Miller Burgoyne.

DEDICATION

To my mother Jo: Thank you for scaring the shit out of me by taking me to see "The Shining" when I was five years old.

To my wife Jenice: This book would not have been possible without your full support. Thank you, for always believing in my storytelling abilities.

And my three children, Sophie, Annabelle and Sebastian: Without all of you the world would be a lot less scary place.

ACKNOWLEDGMENTS

I would like to thank my editor Cindy, for making this book quite a bit easier to read. If there are any lingering items of concern, then I assure you that they were the fault of the author and not the editor. I need to learn to leave well enough alone after the "final" edit is completed.

I would also like to thank Cathy Miller Burgoyne for her wonderful cover art. She created a cover for this book that far exceeded my expectations.

A special thanks to Duc. You know what you did. And thank you for that.

Friday, September 14, 2012

Today sucked ass royally.

This morning I thought it was going to be a Friday like any other. I'd go into work, pretend to work most of the day and attempt to sneak out a half hour to an hour early to get a head start on drinking for the weekend. Best laid plans and all that, right? When I got to work, the first thing I noticed was that the parking lot was half empty, which is extremely odd, since I am not one of the early birds in the office. I shrugged it off as I pulled into a parking spot only eight cars from the front entrance. Bonus! I usually have to park on the side of the building, walking most of the way around to get inside, compounding my usual tardiness. The day started well. I walked into the office at 7:58AM, or so said the large digital clock above the receptionist's desk. It takes me three minutes to walk to my desk, and yes, I have timed this. I have to walk by my boss' office on the way to my cubicle and, lo and behold, The Dragon Lady (as I not so lovingly call her) was not there. The overhead fluorescents in her office, that always give her a sinister glow, were not on. She wasn't in yet. I got to my desk and pressed the power button on the computer. The boss wasn't in yet and I was at my desk a good five minutes earlier than usual. That magical combination would easily be good for getting out at least fifteen minutes early. I didn't even see the office narc, Stacy, when I walked by her cube. Yep, it was going to be a great day.

As my computer was booting up, I walked from my cubicle to the "kitchen," an afterthought of a room if I ever saw one. It likely started out as a closet since it is a five foot by five foot square. The counter ran the entire length of one wall and protruded two feet into the room. The coffee pot sat empty on the counter top, so I started a pot and stood there waiting for it to finish. I love making the coffee (though admittedly I don't usually get there early enough to do it), since it is a legitimate excuse to delay the start of my work by about ten minutes. And believe it or not, staring at the stream of coffee slowly filling the pot is more interesting than balancing spreadsheets, which is what I would have to do when I returned to my desk.

My coffee cup full, I walked out of the kitchen and realized how quiet it was in the office. For a Friday, there was very little chatter around the large room I shared with about twenty other cube dwellers. I looked around and saw only six other people in the room. Five of the six managers' offices were empty and dark. This really is going to be a great day! I meandered through the cube farm back to my desk. I set my coffee cup down, reluctantly sat in my uncomfortable chair and stared at my computer monitor. A screen full of spreadsheet and word processing icons stared back at me. I would have to clean up that mess soon or I would run out of room on the desktop. That sounded like a great time killer for after lunch. I never did get to that.

The first thing I did was open my email and watch as it loaded messages I had received since I left yesterday. As I watched them load, it surprised me to see a lot more than usual. Normally I have two or three from The Dragon Lady asking if I finished the project she gave me at quarter to five the afternoon before. But this morning there was only one of those. I sighed as that first email popped onto my screen with a 5:13PM timestamp from the night before. Then the string of emails from the receptionist began:

Time	From	Subject
5:13PM	Dragon Lady	Did you finish that project?
7:25AM	Mary Tucker	James Ripple is sick and won't...
7:31AM	Mary Tucker	Frank James is sick and won't...
7:40AM	Mary Tucker	Julie Hinijosa is sick and...
7:48AM	Mary Tucker	Bill Stevers is sick and won't...
7:55AM	Mary Tucker	Martina Rodriguez and Diana...
8:03AM	Elizabeth Mart...	WTH!?!?

There were seven more after that. All were letting the office know that so-and-so was going to be out sick today, including one stating that The Dragon Lady wasn't going to be around to hassle me today. When I saw that one, I actually did a little happy dance in my chair.

I clicked on Elizabeth's email, since it was the only one that could potentially have anything interesting in it.

From: Elizabeth Martinez

To: Stephen Macon

Subject: WTH!?!?

Everyone is sick. How are you feeling? This is weird.

I clicked on the reply button and a new email window opened. I stopped right there. Liz sits in the cube right next to mine, yet if I actually speak more than six words to her out loud, The Dragon Lady will shout out her office door, "What are you working on Stephen?" But The Dragon Lady wasn't in. So I walked around the cube walls and stood next to Liz' desk.

Here is where I confess my sexual desire for the Latina Goddess I sit next to day in and day out. (And yes, I had the geek's fantasy that somehow she would read this blog and confess her like desire for me, saving me the horror of rejection.) Liz was about five feet three inches tall. She had gorgeous chestnut colored skin that never faded. Either she was naturally that shade or she tanned on a regular basis. There was a happy thought: Are there tan lines hidden under those clothes? Her jeans were skin tight from waist to ankle, and I could easily imagine her needing help to get them on... or off. She was wearing a loose green blouse over the top of a matching, tight tank top. The cleavage created by the low-cut top was amazing. I continued my hurried visual assessment of her outfit and met her eyes. Hazel ovals blinked at me, accompanied by a knowing smirk. Her eyes were green-tinted today, probably due to the color of her top. She knew I had just checked her out, and she seemed to like it. I internalized a sigh of desire. No one makes casual Friday look so good.

"Steve, what's going on? Everyone is out sick." she said, the smirk fading to a concerned look. Before I could answer, her computer dinged and she looked down at the email that had just arrived. "George is going home; his wife is sick and needs help with their kids. Steve, this is weird."

"I have no idea, Liz. A late summer flu, maybe? Those can be nasty sometimes. I didn't hear anything on the news this morning." I said this, but the truth is I listened to my iPod on the drive in and hadn't turned on the TV at all while getting ready. "It will probably all blow over by Monday, but the news stations will feed everyone's fears about a super swine or avian flu. Who knows? Even The Dragon Lady is out today." Hold the phone, The Dragon Lady is out sick? I think the planets aligned for a second there, because I decided on the spot to throw the 'Hail Mary'. And before I knew exactly what I was going to say, I blurted out, "The Dragon

Lady isn't here, and neither is your boss, you want to sneak out at three thirty or so and grab a happy hour cocktail?"

I did it! I can't believe I actually asked her out. Ok, maybe it wasn't a date, but it was the closest I have ever been able to come to asking her out. And do you know what I got for my bravery?

A vibrant smile lit Liz' face. When she smiled, it wasn't just with her mouth. It really was with her entire face. Her eyes flashed bright green before settling back to a hazel with just a hint of green. Her lips parted and I couldn't believe the words that came out of her mouth then.

"That sounds like a great idea. Now stop checking me out and get back to work. I've got a lot to do today, and since there is no one else around to interrupt me, I am going to get a lot done between now and three thirty."

Can you say, "best day ever?" I knew you could. This day really was starting to look like the best day ever! Barring something major that is.

Did I say something major? Yep. I did. Lunch hour came and went. I really enjoyed those 90 minutes. Then there I was, quietly playing Sudoku on my phone when I heard, "Steve?" in a choked voice from through the cubicle wall.

"Liz? Are you alright?" I stood and peeked over the cube wall into Liz' 'yard'. I always feel like Wilson from that TV show *Home Improvement* when I do that. What I saw when I looked into her space was frightening. Liz wasn't a chestnut brown, she was pale. And pale on her looked very gray.

She looked up at me and opened her mouth, "I think I got food poisoning, Ste..." and her head crashed down on her keyboard hard enough to dislodge the shift key and send it bouncing away.

"Holy shit, Liz!" I leapt out of my cube and ran around to hers. I lifted her head from the keyboard and saw a thin cut above

10

her right eye. Oddly, there was only one drop of blood dripping from the inch long cut. "Oh shit." I lifted her arm and checked her wrist for a pulse. It was weak but there. Her breath was barely perceptible. I was scared. I guess that is how I was able to just act. I lifted her out of the chair and carried her with one of her arms over my shoulder and my arms around her back and behind her knees. I carried her out of the building and to my car. I only stopped long enough to bark at the receptionist, "Mary, call HR, tell them that I'm taking Liz to the hospital and have them call her emergency contact."

Mary listened well and didn't delay me with any questions. Traffic was light for a Friday afternoon and I was able to get to the hospital in record time. The orderlies got Liz out of my car, I told them all I knew, and that she thought it was food poisoning. Liz' family was already in a panic in the waiting room. I retold everything I knew while in the ER waiting room. As we sat there, all the seats slowly began to fill. A lot of individuals looking pale and a couple of them actually passing out just like Liz. At that point, I got really scared. I scribbled my cell number on the back of my business card, handed it to Liz' mom and said, "I've got to get going. I have a work teleconference at 4pm. Please call me when you find out what's wrong." She thanked me for bringing her Lizzy in and hugged me. Then I bugged the hell out of there.

I tried calling the office to give them an update on Liz' condition but the phone just rang six times and went to voicemail. I tried three more times with the same result. So much for doing the right thing. I decided I needed that drink with or without Liz and drove straight to PJ's Pub. I walked through the door at exactly 3:30pm according to my cell phone. I got my wish and got out of work early. Not exactly how I wanted to accomplish it, but the "work gods" work in mysterious ways indeed.

I looked around the gloomy bar and there was only one other person in sight. A woman of about fifty-five, sat at the other end of the bar, holding her bottle of Pabst Blue Ribbon in both hands and staring off into space. I wondered if she had been there since the bar opened at noon. I'd have put money on yes. Other than the resident bar hag, the place was deserted. This couldn't be normal for a Friday afternoon. San Antonians are known for skipping work early on Fridays in order to kick off their weekend right. I was starting to freak out and was about to stand up and walk out the door when Jessica came out of the kitchen.

Jessica is the blonde, blue-eyed bartender whom I could easily picture running down the beach in the opening credits of *Baywatch*. She must have heard me come in. She smiled at me, "How you doin' hun?"

"I'm okay Jess. How 'bout yourself?"

"I'm fantastic. Hoping it picks up in here for happy hour though. This is a tad depressing. What can I get for ya, Sweetie? The usual?"

"Yep, make it a double to start off today, please? Rough day." The usual for me is a Maker's on the rocks.

She poured me a nice full tumbler of that golden nectar of the gods and sat down on a beer cooler that was right behind the bar in front of where I was sitting. I took the first sip of the whiskey and looked into Jessica's bright blue eyes. Jess proceeded to ask me why my day was so bad. I recounted my afternoon, and she really seemed interested (even called me sweet and awesome at different points). The telling of that story turned into her filling me in on her week since I had last been there. The next time I looked at the clock it read 5:43pm. I had consumed three Maker's on the rocks (only one of them was the monster double). I laid two twenties on the bar and bid her adieu. She didn't even look at the money. She pooched out her bottom lip, came around the bar and gave me a big hug.

"You drive careful, hero. Come back tomorrow night and see me. I work eight to close."

"You know, I might just do that. You take care tonight beautiful," I said and walked out the bar door.

I stopped at the liquor store on the way home and bought a bottle of Maker's, intending to have one more while I play on the computer, write my daily blog (which you are reading right now) and maybe watch a movie on Netflix. As I write this, I have accomplished the drink (and a second), surfed the web a bit – the usual: Facebook, Twitter, Gmail, Yahoo! Mail – and now, finally, I am writing. There does seem to be a flu bug hitting all of Texas hard right now. It is all anyone can talk about on Facebook and Twitter. At least I feel fine. And I am confident that the whisky has killed any germs I may have picked up in the emergency room. I have completely wasted four hours sitting here now, and I am going to finish this sentence and go to bed.

Good Night Cyberspace and Cyberspace Readers

Saturday, September 15, 2012 12:30pm

I got up this morning and I felt great. I slept in until 11 and hopped on the treadmill for forty-five minutes. Made myself a three egg omelet with bell peppers, bacon and cheddar cheese. Now I have to run a few errands - grocery store, Lowes for shelving materials and I'll probably stop by the hospital to check on Liz. More later...

4pm

What the hell? I don't know what to write. Liz is dead. Just like that. She never regained consciousness last night. The doctors told me it was the flu. The hospital was in chaos. The entire staff was in a near panic. I heard one nurse say that every room was full and that people were on gurneys in the halls. Again I ask, what the hell? The government says on the TV that there is a new strain of highly virulent flu running wild. Judging by the state of the hospital, I am going to believe it. That explains why the grocery store was so slow today. If only I had heard the news before going there, I would have stocked up on more essentials.

9pm

I just called PJ's and Jess is there. She sounded in a bit of a panic. That seems to be going around lately. (Note to self - find a new word for panic). I'm going to head over there and see if I can help her. I know I can use a drink. And I am not getting anything done here today. I can't get my mind off Liz. I don't understand. I carried her. I don't feel sick. God, I hope it stays that way. The news hasn't been good. People are dying mere hours after they start to feel sick. I don't know why I am considering going out. I just don't feel like being alone right now.

11:30pm

I just got back from PJ's. By the time I got there, Jess was quite a mess. She had been watching the TV in the empty bar. The reports are not good from all around the nation. People are dying by the thousands from whatever this flu is. I am way freaked out myself. I gave Jess my number and told her to call me if she needed to talk. I helped her shut down the bar. She tried to get a hold of the owner before doing so but couldn't reach him on the phone. She is assuming the worst. I followed her home just to make sure she made it there safe and sound. I assured her that I would be up for a while if she needed anything. I'm not sure that is going to be the truth however. I am emotionally drained now. Plus, I am not ashamed to admit, I am quite scared. I can't reach anyone on the phone. I know that during a disaster the phone systems get jammed and calls get that "all circuits are busy" recording. But this is not like that at all. It's as if the circuits are wide open because there is no one left to use them. I kept reaching voice mailbox after voice mailbox. My mother and aunt in Washington didn't answer. I left them voice mails. My cousins in Utah didn't answer. I left them voice mails as well. I tried a couple of friends here in San Antonio, also with no luck.

Facebook traffic has been insane. It is quite a bit lighter than usual, but the few that are posting are all posting about relatives and friends dying all around them. No one seems to be posting about being sick however. It seems like this flu is killing people too fast for them to tell about it themselves. According to the news the flu isn't isolated to just South Texas. People are dying all over the country. And there are reports of flu related deaths all over the world. I am upgrading my question. What the FUCK!? How could this hit everywhere in the world at once like this? Is it terrorism on a global scale? I don't want to sound paranoid, but what the fuck else could it be? I've read plenty of horror novels and watched plenty of horror movies in my life, and this is really starting to feel like one of them. It is starting to feel like something straight out of the mind of Stephen King. Now if I start dreaming about a hundred and six year old black woman sitting on her porch in Nebraska, I will know I woke up in the *Twilight Zone* yesterday. Enough speculation for now. I'm going to watch the news until I fall asleep.

Sunday, September 16, 2012 4:30am

If the circumstances weren't so fucked up, I would be writing this with great excitement right now. Jessica is asleep in my bed next to me. I told her I wouldn't sleep until she got up in a few hours. This has really turned into a nightmare. We are essentially barricaded in my apartment, and I don't know what the fuck is going on outside.

Let me go back a bit.

I walked into my bedroom to lay down around one o'clock. All of the TV stations had given way to the Emergency Broadcast System by then. It was the same message broadcasting on every channel. **"Stay inside. Avoid contact with others. Marshall Law has been instituted nationwide. Stay tuned for further instructions."** This message was even plastered on the Discovery Channel. I tried the radio and it assaulted my ears with this same message repeated up and down the tuner. I found one station that was still on the air; unfortunately, it was a Spanish station. I could only make out one in twenty words or so. Those words that I did make out weren't encouraging either. The DJ was talking so fast and he couldn't keep the terror out of his voice. I heard "muerto" and "apocalipsis" and I think I even heard "zombie". As entertaining as listening to the raving Mexican was, I decided to try to go to sleep.

Jessica called around 1:30am. I had been lying awake contemplating the events of the past thirty-six hours when the phone made me just about jump out of my skin. I grabbed my cell phone and accepted the call even though I didn't recognize the number. She was frantic. It took me a minute to figure out who was screaming at me through the phone. She was ranting something about men trying to get in and the police not answering. I told her to calm down and tell me what was happening. She took a deep breath and started over a little calmer. It was about this point that I recognized her voice. She said there were some people trying to get into her apartment. She used the word zombies. That word flipped a switch in my brain. Thousands dying, and now zombies? I couldn't bring myself to believe it. My buddy, Jake, and I had spent countless hours preparing for the "inevitable" zombie apocalypse when we were kids. I refused to believe it was actually happening. I got her to tell me that her place was locked and that she locked herself in the back bedroom. I told her I was coming to get her and that I would stay on the phone the entire way to her place. Best laid plans right?

Well, it turns out that the word she and that terrified Mexican on the radio had used was indeed correct. Everyone that had died? Yeah, they were up and walking around now. They are pretty slow moving. Thank God (or whomever) for that small miracle. I had grabbed my softball bat before leaving the apartment and I went out into the dark. I gotta tell you that when faced with this event, no amount of disaster preparedness is enough. There were 'people' walking around inside my apartment complex. Inside the gate. Shrouded in shadows I sensed movement from every direction. Luckily, I parked close to my front door and there were none of them (are they really dead?) between the door and Xena, my Xterra. Jess was either calmer or she was going into shock. I got into my car and locked all the doors with the push of one button. I turned the key and slammed the gear into reverse without pausing. I hit the gas and backed up 15 feet, threw it into drive and sped through the complex avoiding the shambling figures as I went. I got to the exit gate and stopped while the sensor detected me and the iron gate slowly slid out of my way. My headlights illuminated the other side of the gate and the way was clear. To my right however, I could see the apartment manager shuffling toward me. At the rate he was moving, I would be out of the gate and it would close behind me before he got to where I was.

Thud, went the hand on my window to the left. It wasn't hard, but it was so sudden that I almost pissed myself. I let out a girlie scream, depressed the gas pedal hard and shot out of the complex. The gate clipped my passenger side mirror on the way through and ripped it clean off the car.

My scream apparently jarred something in Jess, as she began to barrage me with questions. I spent the entire drive to her apartment trying to calm her down again. Her complex wasn't gated. I had been planning to go in, calm her down and maybe just hang out there for the night until we figured out what the hell was going on. I immediately changed my mind. First, her apartment complex wasn't gated and mine was. I needed to feel safe until I came up with a plan. Bars and a gate seemed like a good start. Second, my apartment was in a suburb and hers was downtown close to the hospital. Two plus two still equals four in my book and I don't want to be anywhere near a morgue if in fact this turns out to be Z-Day. All of a sudden, it was a rescue mission. I tried to get all of this across to Jessica en route, but she didn't seem very responsive to the idea of leaving her home.

When I got to her place, it was worse than I had feared. They were everywhere. And to top it off, I heard breaking glass through the phone followed by Jess screaming that they were getting into her living room. I told her to calm down and try to be quiet until I got to her. The only good thing about this whole scenario was the fact that she lived on the bottom floor at the front of the complex. Good and bad, I suppose. Good that I could drive right up to her front door, and bad that it was stop number one for 'them'.

I pulled into the parking lot and saw where her apartment was located. There were about twenty of 'them' in front of her window pushing their way in. A couple of them fell over forward into Jess' apartment because they didn't have the wherewithal to step over the sill. It seemed like we had the intellectual advantage at least. One good thing. My headlights lit them up and they took notice. Almost as one, they all turned and started shambling toward my SUV. I told Jess to be ready, and when I honked my horn from right outside her living room, to come running. She was frantic, and I had a hard time convincing her to agree to this. Eventually she agreed. I had an idea. I explained it to her and sat in my idling vehicle as the zombies made their slow way toward my SUV. My heart was racing in my chest. I'm sure it would have exploded right out if I had heard another thud on my window. This time I kept an eye out both side windows and my rear view, watching the zombies (okay, I fucking said it, they are zombies) shamble closer. I counted down into the phone from ten to one. While doing this I primed my nerves for what was next. When I got to one, I slammed down on the gas and shot forward. The first zombie went down without flinching as I hit it with the front end of my car. The next did the same. Several glanced off to either side and I hit the curb bouncing up onto the grass. I almost lost control of Xena then and had to take my foot off the gas. I slowed and bounced over a few more of them and slammed my foot down on the brake, skidding to a halt about two yards from Jess' broken living room window. At the same time, I laid on the horn and screamed into the phone for her to get out here NOW!!!

I expected this part to be more difficult. She apparently hadn't waited for the horn. She was out the window and reaching for the passenger handle mere seconds after I stopped. I threw the phone down when I saw her.

"Get in Jess! Get in!" I screamed at her as she tried the handle and I tried to look every direction at once.

"I can't!" she screamed back at me. "It's locked!"

"Fuck!" I reached for the button and the door unlocked and flew open at once. She jumped in with one last look behind the vehicle. She screamed and slammed the door shut behind her.

"You asshole! Get us out of here! Go!" and she slapped me on the shoulder.

Not all of this really registered at the time. I was already putting the car in reverse and backing up as fast as I could. A few zombies went under in the process and we got out of there.

There was no one on the road. No vehicles at least. Was it because there wasn't anyone else alive? Or was I the only one stupid enough to go out? I'm guessing at this point that the latter is the more likely. Damn my overinflated sense of chivalry. That was the last time. Jake and I always said, "Chivalry will get you killed." We got back to my apartment complex quickly and into the gate easily enough. There were more zombies shuffling about, but not nearly as many as at Jess'. I pulled my car all the way up to my front door. Fuck parking places now. I didn't have to use the bat at all. We got in the front door and went up the stairs to the left into my living room. I have never been happier in my life not to live on the bottom floor. I propped a dining room chair under the handle of the door just to make myself feel better. A little bit anyway.

Now I have a sleeping beauty, pun definitely intended, in bed next to me and an uncertain future ahead of me (us?).

Fuck, what a day! It is probably best not to think too much about the future right now. I need to sleep. One thing I know: No more chivalry!

Sunday, September 16, 2012 8am

When I opened my eyes, I was still sitting up in bed. My neck and back were very stiff from sleeping sitting up with my head resting on my left shoulder for... how long? I lifted my head and a sharp pain shot through my neck. I hissed in a quick breath of air to compensate for the pain. I slowly rolled my head in a full circle to loosen up my neck. My eyes absently took in the room. My gaze paused on the alarm clock on the dresser next to my bed. The big red display told me it was 7:43. Why had I gotten only three hours sleep? Why was I sleeping sitting up?

Then the events of the night and early morning flooded back into my brain like a dam bursting. My breathing became a pant as if the flood of memories was threatening to drown me. I tried to calm myself and finished my head roll looking at the bed next to me. There was a hot little blonde bartender sound asleep not even a foot away from me. The rescue mission hit me hard, and in the early morning light, it didn't seem like such a horrible idea. At least not until I relived the events in my head. The drive to her place. The frantic escape from her place and return here. Calming her down and putting her to bed. Did I really sit up next to her innocently as if she were my sister or something? It would appear that I had. Damnit, what the hell was wrong with me? I slid out of bed and went into the bathroom. I splashed water onto my face. I toweled off the cold water and stood staring into the mirror surveying myself.

"Oh God, what is going on?" I didn't expect an answer, nor did I get one. So I went back into my bedroom, grabbed my laptop and slipped into the adjacent living room.

Ok, what the fuck?! How is this for a fucked up situation? I've got a woman that I have had impure thoughts about for almost three years now sleeping in my bed. It is not even eight in the morning and I am sitting in the living room trying to figure out what the fuck is going on in this town. This state? This country? Fuck. Every channel on TV is either still on the emergency broadcast alert or they are simply broadcasting snow. So, here I am writing and trying to find some reliable news on the 'net'.

Well, that was interesting. CNN reports that this is going on all over the US and is in fact happening all over the world. They are trying not to use the word zombie. I guess it is a word that serious journalists don't use. They can call 'them' whatever they want, but I know what the deal is. Thank you, George Romero, for preparing me for this. The reports say that the dead are indeed trying to eat the living, and to avoid them at all costs. They are particularly dangerous in large numbers. Basically, the situation is exactly as in the classic zombie movies. I didn't need CNN to tell me any of this. I had experienced it firsthand the night before when I went out to help Jess. The report says they are fairly easy to avoid as long as there aren't many of them around. There are estimates that upwards of seventy-five percent of the population died in the initial outbreak. Those of us still alive are cautioned against venturing outside and advised to barricade ourselves in our homes. I don't like the sound of that very much, especially since I don't know when, or even if, help is going to come. The report was not encouraging as far as letting us know what is being done about this either. The military suffered the same losses as the civilian sector. So judging by what I saw at work yesterday, help isn't going to be coming any time soon. There are reports that some of 'them' are able to move about more rapidly, but nothing seemingly faster than a brisk walk. We are told to avoid them and anyone who has recently been ill. That is where this seems to have started. Whatever this is, it began with all those sick people. Liz... I hope you are resting in peace.

I've got enough food and water for myself for about five days. Of course, if Jess stays, then that is cut in half. Ok, so I need to figure out a plan. I will keep trying to connect with...

A blood-curdling scream came from my bedroom. The laptop tumbled to the floor, landed thankfully on the bottom and not on the monitor. I jumped up and ran into the next room. What I saw was inexplicable. Jess was still in bed and there was another person standing by the window. The sunlight streamed in behind whoever it was. I jumped to the side of the bed, reached for Jess and found only a jumble of sheets and blankets.

I breathed out a "Huh?" and stole a look down. Empty. The sheets and blankets had just made it look like someone was in the bed. I looked back up at the figure across the room. The second time my brain processed the scene before me. It was Jessica standing at the window looking out. She had her hands up to her face and was trembling from head to toe. Then a whimper escaped her.

The chivalrous knight awoke in me again with the whimper. I ran around the bed, turned her to face me and held her to me. I put her head on my chest. I looked outside and saw a horrific scene unfolding below. Apparently, a woman had gotten caught by one of the zombies and was struggling to escape as he tore at her flesh. From just about everywhere I looked there were more of them moving in to share in the kill like a shambling clan of hyenas.

Jessica was murmuring into my chest. I turned her around and stepped her back the three or so steps to the bed. I guided her to sit on the edge of the bed; she would not let go of me and we almost fell over. Under any other circumstance, I would have gone with it. In this case, I wanted her away from the window and to be free from her so I could see the rest of the scene below. I didn't really want to see what was going on. But I felt I needed to know what we were dealing with here in the light of day.

"Shhhhhhh, calm down Jess"" I said. "I need to see what's going on out there. I need to know how bad it is."

"He got her," she shouted into my chest. "Just caught hold of her hair as she tried to run by him and he caught her hair and down she went. Then he started biting her. Stephen, how can this be happening? I don't understand!" She began to sob against me.

I stopped trying to push her away from me. I held her tight against me and turned her with her back to the window so I could look out over her shoulder. And boy was it gruesome. I've seen my fair share of zombie movies since my childhood. What I was looking at could have easily been a scene out of any of those movies. I saw at least seven zombies - men and women - on their knees scrambling to get their hands into the poor woman's soft flesh. Chunks of flesh hanging out of their mouths as they greedily tried to seize their next bite before they had even finished swallowing what was in their mouth. There were intestines strung out and gnawed into. When they ripped her colon free and the black feces spilled onto one zombie's chest, I had to force down my gag reflex. There were more zombies coming. The seven already feeding were about to have the company of half a dozen more.

I tore my eyes away from the grisliness below to survey the visible part of my complex. I was relieved to see there were only a couple more of them within my sight line. The bad part was that all of them were right outside my front door.

"Jess, we have to stay put for a couple days. Hopefully the national guard or the army or whoever will have this taken care of by then." I couldn't bring myself to tell her what the article had said about the military. "I've got enough food for a few days. I'm going to need your help now to get everything we need ready. Can you do that for us? She shook her head violently without looking up at me.

"Come on Jessica. Look at me." I placed my hands on the side of her head and tilted her face up to mine. Her eyes were closed so tight that her entire face was squished together. Definitely not attractive.

"Jessica honey, please open your eyes and look at me. I need you. I need you to hear me. I need you to help me. Please." I didn't know what I would do if that didn't work, but it did. I watched her face relax. Then her eye sockets. Then her eyelids began to flutter and slowly open. She looked up at me with her watery blue eyes. I could see the fear and pleading on her face as she stared intently at me. Into me almost.

"Is this a nightmare?" She asked as the first tears started to stream from her eyes.

"No, honey. But we're going to be alright. This will hopefully be over within a couple days, now that the government knows what it's dealing with. And now that *we* know what we're dealing with we can prepare. Make sense? I have emergency supplies, but I need your help to get this place ready. Can you do that for me?" My eyes never once left hers. I willed her to be soothed by my steady gaze and calm voice. (Hey, it's my blog, I can be the suave and handsome hero if I want to be.)

"Now, I need you to go into my spare bedroom closet and get my toolbox, please. Bring it here. And try to stay away from the windows." I could actually see her steel herself from the inside out. She let go of me, turned and walked from my room.

When she had gone, I stole one more glance out the window and saw the mess. There wasn't much left of that poor woman; a litter of picked clean bones. The zombies started to wander away from the remains in search of more food. I went to work gathering the things I needed.

8pm

Let's see if I can recap the day. Jessica was awesome today. She was jumpy, but she understood that there were things we needed to do. Our first order of business was to make the only door into the apartment as secure as possible but we also had to be able to open it in a hurry.

My apartment layout is simple. Walk in the front door and there are stairs immediately up to the left. Essentially, it's a hallway up to the second floor. This made it easy to barricade the door to my liking. I made a little too much noise, but not as bad as it could have been. I tore my bed apart for the materials I needed to make the barricade. That was the sturdiest source of wood I could find in my apartment. I cut the shelf from my headboard into four U-shaped pieces about six inches on each side. I was going to secure these to the door and the wall opposite the door, when I realized the opposite wall wouldn't provide enough support unless the key points on the door were exactly lined up with studs in the wall. A quick check with the stud finder told me that wasn't the case. That meant I had to somehow reinforce the wall before attaching the 'U's', or find a way to distribute any force from the door. After ten minutes of wandering through the apartment, I finally found something I could use. The sides off my spare computer worked perfectly. Yeah, they are only aluminum, but better than drywall, and with any luck, I won't have to find out if they are good enough. They are wide enough that I could attach them to the studs. After those were secured to the wall, I screwed the 'U's' to them. Two directly across from the doorknob about one third and two thirds up the height of the door. Two screwed into the metal door across from the computer case sides. I had to do all this by hand to make the least amount of noise possible. I looked out the peephole every once in a while and only when I was finished with the 'U's' did I see any of them out there.

There were two that seemed like they were trying to find the source of the noise. I don't think I breathed for two minutes while I watched them. My neighbor's front door is perpendicular to my own and they must have thought the sound was coming from behind that door. The zombie outside my door didn't look like a zombie in the movies. He was neither decomposing nor covered with blood. He just looked extremely pale and emaciated. It looked like all the blood in him had evaporated and his skin had sunken into the spaces voided by blood. Then another joined him. This one walked up to the large window next to the neighbor's front door. This one was a woman in a nightgown. She put one hand up on the glass and began to push on it. As I watched, she pushed and released. She apparently sensed a weakness in that point of entry because she began to push harder on the glass. After a few moments, she began pounding on the glass. Luckily for my neighbors (if they are alive and at home) the windows in this complex are double paned and very sturdy. The zombie in the nightgown just kept pounding away.

The first zombie saw her doing this and joined her in pounding on the glass. I don't think I could have kept my sanity if that were my apartment. One thing I noticed was that they were not making any noise. The only sound I heard was the persistent pounding on the glass. There was no moaning. There were no comical pleas for "Braaaaaains." Nothing.

I turned from the peephole and grabbed the tape measure. I measured the distance between the 'U's' on the door and the 'U's' on the wall. I quietly walked up the stairs and when I got to the top, Jess was kneeling in front of the window peering through the blinds. I walked over to her, knelt down next to her and put one hand on her shoulder. She jumped and let out a little squeak. She whirled and faced me with her hands up, ready to defend herself. I flinched and raised my hands as well to ward off the inevitable attack. It didn't come. She let out a breath and turned back to the window after slapping me on the shoulder and giving me a look that would have stopped a charging rhino.

"There are more of them out there now," she said. "I've only seen one car go by the whole time you've been working. It was hauling ass toward downtown. Why would anyone head in that direction? I'd be hauling ass out of town. Speaking of... why aren't we trying to get the hell out of here?" She turned from the window again and looked at me.

"We don't have a grasp on how bad things are yet. I don't know if we are going to get a handle on it. I don't like the idea of being trapped here any more than you do. I am not ready to face what is going on out there just yet, though. I want to assess as best I can. See if we can gather any more info before venturing out. Do *they* seem the same as earlier? Any change?"

"No. They're still just milling around out there. The gate out there hasn't opened since I've been watching. So all the ones on the outside are still outside and the ones inside are still inside." She turned toward me and her face hardened. "Do you have a gun?"

"No, I think I may be the only man in Texas who doesn't own a gun." I looked like a big baby while saying that, I'm sure. But lying would get us nowhere fast. I obviously wish now I was one of those gun-toting rednecks who permeate South Texas. My first thought was, *I'm a liberal Californian who believes in gun control, don't you wish you had stayed in your apartment now? Oh no, of course not, because if you had done that you'd be dead right now.* Of course I couldn't say that. I knew she wasn't accusing me of anything. She was merely asking me a simple question. I decided to take her mind from that and back to other forms of defense. "Would you help me cut the braces? I've finished the mounting slots for them. It shouldn't take long, and then we should be pretty secure in here. At least until…"

The front door handle jiggled. We both turned toward the stairs and the front door. It jiggled again. I moved for the 2X4's I had taken from the frame of my bed, grabbed the tape measure, measured out the length and started cutting. The handsaw cut painfully slow. I didn't want to use power tools because of the noise they made. In the silence that had fallen over the world in the last twenty-four hours any little sound seemed to reverberate. The handsaw was excruciatingly loud in my ears. I could only hope that the insulation in this apartment would keep it from reaching *their* ears. But with safety an issue, I couldn't afford not to chance it. Cutting through the board seemed to take forever. When the saw broke through the last few slivers of wood and fell to the floor, I grabbed the measured piece of wood and rushed as quietly as I could down the stairs. When I got to the bottom, the door handle jiggled again.

I slid the board down into the "U's" two thirds of the way up. For perhaps the first time in my life, I was not disappointed with my carpentry skills. I had to stifle a giddy laugh. I hurried back up the stairs and Jessica greeted me at the top with a length of board that had been cut on one end. It looked about right. I didn't ask, I only walked back down the stairs and placed it in the lower set of "U's". I climbed the stairs again to find Jessica standing there with her arms crossed under her breasts looking back at me. The question on her face didn't need to be asked. I answered it, "All done and there is no way they are getting in that way." She took a deep breath and the concern on her face faded to a weak smile. *Damn she's HOT!* I'm just saying. "Thank you for your help Jess. I really appreciate it. My arms are on fire from having to do all that without power tools. May I get you some water? I need a short break before we get back to work."

To my surprise, she sat on the couch next to me and took one of my hands. "Stephen, thank you for coming to get me last night. I don't think I would be alive today if you hadn't. I don't know why it was worse at my place than here, but I will be here to help you in any way I can until this thing is over, whenever that may be. Just tell me what you want me to do. I am indebted to you. Thank you, thank you, thank you." And she kissed my hand, and then my cheek.

Well, since my life isn't a Harlequin romance novel – come to think of it, my life is now a horror movie – I didn't score. I didn't even think of sex as repayment for saving her. I was really only thinking about staying alive. How lame am I? Oh well. It doesn't look like we are leaving here for a while. Who knows, maybe tomorrow…

We spent the rest of the day inventorying my food supplies. Then I actually decided to clean my toilets and bathtubs (I have two of each). I explained to Jess that we would eventually lose running water, and I wanted the tubs and toilets full of clean water when that happened. She understood and cleaned one of the bathrooms. After rinsing the basins thoroughly, we filled them completely with fresh water.

The sun is going down and it is time to call it a day. I don't want to have the lights on after dark. I don't know much about *them* yet. Maybe that is what I will do tomorrow - begin my research. The more I know about them, the better our chances of survival, right? Now the daylight is about gone, so I am going to log off and shut down the computer. I hope the power is still on tomorrow. I am printing this account just in case. Good night all. I think I may be sleeping beside a hot bartender again tonight.

Monday, September 17, 2012 9am

Wow, over ten hours sleep. I feel completely rested and ready for the day. I know you are wondering (assuming you still have internet and electricity where you are) if I got lucky with the beautiful Jessica last night. I would love to say yes, but the farthest I got was a goodnight kiss and a request for me to hold her since she was scared. I'm glad I could comfort her. Now who the fuck is going to comfort me? Fuck chivalry.

On tap for today: prepare 'bug out bags' - essentials that will help us survive at least a couple days on the road in case we need to get the hell out of here in a hurry. I know my Xterra's gas tank is about three-quarters full (which is only going to get us a little more than two hundred miles from here at best. It already has a full first aid kit in it, so I will focus on the non-medical supplies.

We are going to need weapons of some kind. I chuckled just now, thinking of "Shaun of the Dead," and I kinda wish I had a cricket bat. I'll have to make do with my aluminum softball bats. How much camping food do I have in the closet? I guess I'll find out. Who knows where we'll be sleeping if we need to get the hell out of Dodge.

Incoming chat request from Studio54Reject691: DUDE YOU THERE??

SNM456: Jake, you alright? And quit yelling!

Studio54Reject691: Steve, what the fuck man? Is it happening in San Antonio too?

SNM456: Yessir. Houston too?

SNM456: You guys ok over there?

Studio54Reject691: Yeah it's here too. It's bad. We haven't left the house in two days. Not since the TV stations here cut out. Power's gone out a couple times and the phones went down before the TV. Janus and the kids are fine.

Studio54Reject691: Dude, I watched the guy across the street get eaten man! WTF!? We haven't left the house since then. Those things are everywhere. We've blockaded the front door and boarded up the windows as best we can.

SNM456: Just stay inside and stay safe. How are your supplies? How about the backyard?

Studio54Reject691: Well, as often as we talked about this day, you'd think we'd be more prepared for it. But with the kids, it has been hard enough to make ends meet, let alone get enough ahead to be able to prepare for a major disaster.

Studio54Reject691: And this is the fucking zombie apocalypse! Not some hurricane or tornado. I never thought I'd rather have one of those.

Studio54Reject691: The backyard is secure so far. I've been out there a couple times. The world is SO quiet dude. The birds are all gone. Where the hell did they all go man? And the movies got it wrong. These fuckers don't moan. They don't make a fucking peep.

There have been a few cars that have torn down our block. And that seems to keep them away from our house. It's like they follow the noise.

SNM456: I noticed how quiet they are. It is fucking creepy.

SNM456: I guess it makes sense tho. Since they are predators, they wouldn't want to announce their presence. Or maybe they lost their vocal abilities. Either way, it's not a good thing for us.

Studio54Reject691: Nice SotD reference. Janus wants me to get off the computer. Do you think we should try to meet up? Do you want to come here? What time do you want to meet online again?

SNM456: You just stay put man. You look after your family. Let me think on this today. Get back online at 6. I don't want the computer light on after dark. We'll figure something out. Stay put and stay safe. And remember what we planned for. If you have to leave before we talk again, leave a note under your pillow letting me know where you tried to go. Let us think this out today. It isn't a long drive under normal circumstances, but under these…

Studio54Reject691: I know man. Just remember everything we talked about pertaining to Z-day.

SNM456: I will, man.

Ok, that adds a new wrinkle to my plan. I need to talk this over with Jess, but if there is one person in the world I would most like to be with during this, it's Jake. I know he seemed panicked, but I know the amount of knowledge in his head. And it is vital. I hope he just keeps it together long enough to ride this out. Now I need to convince Jess. Fuck, Houston is 200 miles away. It might as well be 2000 miles. The TV showed massive traffic leaving the city before the stations went off the air. Most of that was to the north and west though.

I just peaked out my office blinds and there are a lot of them outside the fence. Some are trying to get in, but most are just wandering aimlessly. Inside is what really concerns me. Apparently a lot of my neighbors died in their apartments because there are a lot of zombies I kind of recognize. Great! I'm glad I pulled Xena up to the front door the other night. We won't have to go very far if we decide to take off. Ok, enough dilly-dallying. It's time to get the bug out bags ready.

5pm

If I know Jake, he'll be on early, so I am going to try to recap the day before he does. First, Jess agreed to go to Houston. I am not entirely positive it is the right choice, but I think I'd prefer it. I'd really like to be around friends if this really is the end of the world. And Jake has always been the best friend I have ever had. I know I said no more chivalry but Jake is a special case. His kids are my god kids and I can't let anything happen to them if I can help it. Jess' only request was to wait a few days to see if this thing ends on its own. I don't think it will, but I must say I feel safe in my little castle at the moment.

We have our bags ready to go. We put together four of them. Two are full of my freeze-dried camping food, one with my camping essentials, including my stove and butane canisters. They are heavy but I only have to carry them as far as the car. One is my backcountry backpack, so it will work nicely if I do have to carry it far. I can rearrange items later if I need to. The fourth bag has nonessentials and is the smallest. I wanted to pack some comforts like deodorant, toothpaste, shampoo, and the like. A little comfort can go a long way for morale later on. This bag also has what little cash I've squirreled away for a zombie apocalypse (any emergency actually). And lo and behold that day is here. I don't know what good it's going to do now, but you never know, right?

I think the canned goods and perishables in the fridge will last us about four days, which I think sets our absolute time limit. Even if the power stays on, we are out of here four days from now. September 21st. The first day of Autumn. That sounds like a perfect day to start an adventure. Hopefully, we are the heroes in this adventure and not some of the expendable victims. As long as we are smart about this, I think we'll be fine. Only time will tell.

Until we leave, I have a hair-brained plan to try to get us more supplies. Tomorrow morning I will tunnel through the wall between my and my neighbor's apartments. Looting? Hell yes! Desperate times call for desperate measures, right? I'll have to be careful though. My neighbor is a cop and I don't want to get shot going through. I will start by pounding on the wall to see if there is any response. If there is none, then I am going for it. If there is a *human* response, then I am going for it. Who knows what I'll find over there. I can see his front door from my living room window and at least it is closed. His downstairs neighbor's door is wide open, so that's not a good sign.

The shamblor activity is steady. No more, no less. I have Jess watching through the blinds and told her to come get me if it seems like there is an opening to get the bags into the car. So far I haven't heard from her. I will just sit here and wait for Jake. It is only 5:30.

Haha, Google is still up and running but a lot of the sites it links me to are not. I was able to find a few survival sites still up and printed out a book worth of shit. Anything I could think of that may help keep *us* alive if we need to live off the land. I've got to get a long-term goal soon. Houston isn't it. I am going to tell Jake that when he…

Studio54Reject691: Steve?

SNM456: Yessir. I'm here. How you doing?

Studio54Reject691: Scared man. They know we're in here. I don't know how, but they are trying to get in. There are about 20 of them, man. They're all quiet and pawing at the glass and the front door.

SNM456: Calm down, Jake.

SNM456: I think they are just guessing. We have the same thing here too. They try to get into an apartment and give up after an hour or so and then wander off to try somewhere else.

SNM456: Just keep your head on. Get your bug out bags ready.

Studio54Reject691: I've tried man, but Janus won't let me.

SNM456: You need to explain to her that it is just a precaution. You need to be ready to get out of there if they get in. Do you have the note under your pillow already?

Studio54Reject691: Yes man, but

SNM456: No

SNM456: You need to do this. How many hours did we spend planning for this? How many hours of mental preparation for something I deep down didn't think would ever really happen. But we did plan for this.

SNM456: Come on man.

Studio54Reject691: Ok, but it ain't gonna be easy.

SNM456: Remember, the key words are JUST IN CASE.

SNM456: got it?

Studio54Reject691: Yeah. Are you safe? Are you coming? I'd really like to have you around man. You were always the calm, cool and collected one. I think it would help our situation.

SNM456: We are going to stick around here a few more days.

Studio54Reject691: You keep saying WE. Who is WE?

SNM456: Shit. I assumed you'd read my blogs since you were still online.

Studio54Reject691: no

SNM456: Remember me telling you about that hot bartender down the road at PJ's?

Studio54Reject691: You didn't tell me you were shacking up with her. WTF?!

SNM456: Long story. I'll tell you in person. It really was a heroic moment on my part. You'll love it.

SNM456: For now, I am going to try to acquire more supplies from my neighbors. And if any of them are alive, I'll be bringing them along.

SNM456: I hope some of them are alive. I want to play hero some more.

Studio54Reject691: Asshole.

SNM456: Ok, here is the plan. We are going to hang out here, lay low and gather as many supplies as we can for a couple days. We have about 4 day's food in the apt. So that would be the latest we would take off.

SNM456: We are going to wait to see if (not sent)

Studio54Reject691: 4 DAYS!?!??! Dude, they will be in by then!

SNM456: Calm down man. Seriously. If you are going to lose it, where will Janus and Maggie and little Jake be?

SNM456: fucked

SNM456: that's where. So calm the FUCK down! Use your head. Do you need me to give you tasks to keep you focused? All I am going to do is remind you of everything we've already talked about. All those nights in your backyard by the fire pit?

Studio54Reject691: FUCK! Ok, I can do this. You have to be smart about this too.

Studio54Reject691: You need to make it here safely. That's what's important. Then we can work together. FUCK! I'm just scared man. My kids.

SNM456: I know, Jake.

SNM456: Our plan. I want to be ready for this trip. It's going to be long and scary for us. I don't want to make a mistake.

SNM456: I am going to try to get supplies and more weapons. Right now, I don't know how to kill these fuckers. I am assuming it is like the movies. But who knows.

SNM456: It may be sooner. We've agreed to wait until our food runs out, and hopefully the army or national guard or whoever (haha) will get it cleaned up before we have to risk our necks and go out there.

SNM456: If the power goes out before then, then we are hitting the road. At next light.

Studio54Reject691: That makes sense.

SNM456: Ok, in the morning I want to check in with you. 10am sound good to you?

Studio54Reject691: Yeah man. That's perfect. We aren't really sleeping well anyway. And tomorrow evening?

SNM456: Same bat time, same bat channel my friend. Now go take care of your family, and first thing in the morning you get your bug out bags ready, *JUST IN CASE*

Studio54Reject691: Just in case. I love you bro. Thank you.

SNM456: Jake, I'll see you soon and talk to you in the morning. I love you man.

That went well. How can he be freaking out that much? The kids I guess. Well, time to start enacting the plan. First a good night's sleep.

Good night cyberspace.

Tuesday, September 18, 2012 9:30am

I didn't sleep well at all. Nightmares about zombies and shit. Go figure. Woke up early. Power is still on obviously, since I am typing this and not hand writing it. The activity outside is a little heavier. I'm starting to recognize more of my neighbors shambling around. The stripper (at least I assume she is, because of how she dresses and her big fake boobs) who lives in the next building is now a zombie. She apparently sleeps in the nude, because she is walking around the parking lot completely in the buff. It took me a minute to recognize her. She was always thin, but now she looks like a concentration camp victim with a boob job. Her implants are no longer sexy. With no blood flowing to the tissue around them (an assumption on my part) they look like two flesh colored water balloons that someone stuffed a pair of old rolled up socks into. She is definitely no longer an object of men's desires. I'd say, she is now truly a man eater. No cars yet this morning down the street. Lots of zombies on the other side of the fence.

Holy shit! The fence. The gate! We can't wait for the power to go out. We need the power on to get out of here easily. If we wait for the power to go out, then I will have to get out of Xena to open the gate by hand. And who knows if I will even be able to? Fuck that! Gotta talk to Jess about that. She's not going to like it.

Ok, about my plan to go through the wall. Since about 6am, I've been knocking on the walls between our apartments, listening, and getting no response. I hope that means no one is home. I'm going to have to use power tools to get over there. I am not looking forward to the noise. Jake was right yesterday. It is quiet. Every sound we make causes me to wince. There haven't been any more attempts at the doorknob though. That's encouraging. But a circular saw is going to make a lot more noise and for a longer period of time than knocking over a tray table. I've done that a couple times already. I don't see a way around it however. At least for the first cut. To hell with it, I am going to find something heavy and use it like a battering ram. All I really need is a hole big enough to wedge in and rip bigger chunks out until it is big enough to fit through. I hope. I'm not a contractor and I've never seen the inside of an apartment wall. These walls do seem thin though. Hopefully, it will be a matter of drywall, insulation, drywall and I'm through. There may be some wiring – another good reason not to saw blindly.

Jess just came in and said there were only two she could see inside the gates from the front window. I told her to keep watch and if those two also disappeared, we would try to quietly load the car. I stood up, gave her a hug and thanked her for keeping an eye on that. I said we had to discuss a few things after I talked with Jake. She said ok and went back to the chair she had pulled to the living room window.

What an odd fucking situation. I'm pretty sure there is no attraction on her part for me. That makes it hard to think of myself as the hero of this story. Oh well. There's other fish in the sea right? Maybe. Shit who knows. Maybe the sea has dried up.

Incoming chat request from Studio54Reject691

Studio54Reject691: Steve. Good morning. How are you two doing?

Um, is this the same Jake? All of a sudden calm, cool and collected?

SNM456: Jake? We're doing fine. How about you four?

Studio54Reject691: We're fine. It's like you said man. They gave up and walked off.

SNM456: This is the Jake I know. Keep it together, man. I want to keep this short. I'm going through the wall as soon as I log off - into the cop's bedroom from my bedroom.

SNM456: Have you worked on your bug out bags?

Studio54Reject691: Yeah man. I told Janus they were just in case and she actually calmed down and helped. I think she thinks I have a plan. I couldn't tell her that I didn't. That I just had you. And that you are the hero of this story.

SNM456: I was just blogging about that.

SNM456: Aren't heroes supposed to get the girl? That ain't happening here.

Studio54Reject691: Dude she may not have much of a choice if this thing continues long. We must repopulate the earth right?

SNM456: Shut up. What time do you want to chat tonight? 6 again?

Studio54Reject691: Yeah. Be careful going through that wall. You don't know what's on the other side.

SNM456: True, but I need to try man. I'll let you know how it went later. Take care until then.

Studio54Reject691: Deal, and Steve, don't let your meat loaf.

SNM456: Good-bye, jackass.

Studio54Reject691 has logged off.

Ok, through the wall I go.

Noon

Fuck, fuck, fuck, fuck. That was some fucked up shit. I went through the wall. What a mess. First of all, it was WAY easier than I figured it would be to get through. One full forced whack with a hammer and I had the hole I needed. Then I yanked chunks of drywall with the claw of the hammer until I had a hole from the floor to just above my head, and from stud to stud on either side. It only took about three minutes. I had to fit through sideways, since I am broader than the sixteen inches from stud to stud. As I was yanking drywall, I was also yanking the pink insulation shit out as well. No wonder I could hear my neighbors fucking all the time. The walls really do consist of drywall, insulation and drywall. It's time to get a house. Oh wait, I might be able to take my pick now.

After I cleared out the space between the drywall, I hit the back of the other wall with the hammer. It went through like it did on my side, but then it hit something on the other side. I was worried it was going to be a big ass bureau or something. It wound up being just a mirror on the wall. My second hit apparently broke the mirror from behind and sprayed shards of glass all over the room. I guess I don't know my own strength. I started to pull chunks of drywall like I had on my side.

I had no warning. There I was breaking off chunk after chunk of drywall and all of a sudden the mirror fell away and my neighbor's little boy appeared and jumped through the hole. The little fucker moved faster than any of the others I'd seen. He jumped onto me. I slipped on a bit of drywall and fell to my back. His teeth gnashed at me. He tried to take a bite out of my arm. I rammed the hammer sideways into his mouth like a horse bit. I heard a crunch, but he didn't seem to register any pain. He just kept trying to take a chunk of flesh from me. I managed to throw him off to the side against the remains of my bed. He was up in a flash, intent on making me his breakfast. He was covered in blood already. He

44

looked similar to the rest of them. Pale skin, with dark shadows around his eyes. He didn't look as emaciated as the ones outside. Of course, I didn't have time to register that at the time. The next thing I knew a baseball bat came into view and collided with the side of the little fucker's head and he went flying off me and landed on the floor next to my bed. Jessica was standing there with a softball bat in a batter's stance after taking a full swing. She just hit one out of the park as far as I was concerned. The boy began to move again. Jess swung the bat over her head and brought it full force on the boy's forehead with a grunt of effort. There was a loud crunch and I could see his head cave in from the force of the blow. This time he fell to the floor and stayed down.

"Jess, thank you. I owe you one."

"No, I call it even now. You got me out of my apartment. Now let's see if there is anything worth this over there. I don't think I want to be here anymore."

I just gawked at her. I pulled myself together and stood up. I looked from her to the remains of the boy on the floor, to the hole in the wall and back to her. "That is actually what I wanted to talk to you about. Let's get this over with, see if we can find any weapons or anything that makes this," I motioned to the mess on my bedroom floor, "worth it."

She nodded and motioned to the hole in the wall. I went back to work on the drywall. This time, more cautiously. I took my time to listen to the room on the other side. That turned out to be a waste of time. There was no one left alive. Nor was there any member of the flesh-eating undead. I finished the man-sized hole, moved the mirror to the side and peered into the room. What a gory sight. My neighbors were in bed, and there was blood everywhere. The little boy had apparently been munching on them for a couple days now. They weren't recognizable as my neighbors. I just assumed it was them.

I surveyed the room quickly and saw no movement. I fully entered the room, my heart racing with fear and adrenaline. I can't believe their little kid did this. The little monster, I corrected myself immediately following this thought. Jess really stepped up and saved my life.

Phil and Patty were on the bed with their insides strewn all about. They were naked as far as I could tell through the blood and chunks of meat. That little shit really did all that. I walked closer to them to make sure they weren't going to get up and come after me. That wasn't going to be an issue. As I got closer, I noticed the two blood and brain splatters on the wall behind and above them. I couldn't understand this at first and I may never fully comprehend it. My best guess is that when their son died they killed themselves. I never would have imagined that he would have done this. He was the stereotypical macho cop. The evidence on the wall told a different story.

Ok, one piece of information learned so far this morning. Braining *them* works to put them down. Now to see what there was to pillage from this apartment. First, find the gun they used. It took a little searching. I found it in the bloody mess between the two of them. I've never been squeamish around blood, but the blood and the smell combined was too much. I don't know how long they had been dead, but the stench was nauseating. It's hard to describe. I've never wondered what the smell was like, but have seen a lot of actors trying to portray their reaction to it on film. It was worse than I could have ever imagined. There was the coppery smell of the blood as well as the smell of shit, no doubt from their ripped-open colons. That thought did it. Picturing that little boy ripping into flesh tubes full of shit caused my stomach to clench and expel its contents onto the floor. My partially digested cereal and milk added to the bloody mess already there.

"Are you alright?" came Jessica's voice from the other side of the wall.

After my stomach finished convulsing, I answered her, "Yeah, just losing my breakfast. It's bad in here. My neighbors killed themselves. Let's try to keep our voices down. Everything sounds so much louder now. Have you noticed that?"

"Yeah, I've noticed. Do you need my help?"

"No, I think I can get out of here in ten minutes. I'll bring everything I find back to you."

"Ok Steve, please be careful. I don't want to lose you."

The compassion in her tone as much as her words lifted my heart. Maybe I can be the hero in this after all – eventually.

The bloody entrails of my neighbors were strewn all over the bed. I reached down between them and grabbed the butt of the gun, taking it to the foot of the bed. I had never held a gun in my life, and it was not nearly as heavy as I expected. I bent down at the end of the bed and used the comforter to wipe the gun off as best I could. I need to look up whether you can get this kind of gun, whatever it is, wet. I need to thoroughly clean it. It was still quite sticky after wiping it off.

I went to the closet first and immediately realized that there was hope for us. I came through the wall hoping to find enough weaponry to arm a militia. Standing open to the left of all the clothes was a massive gun safe. It wasn't the National Guard armory I wanted, but it was more than I had for sure. There was another handgun, I think it's called a glock – I have to look it up. A shotgun – of that I am sure. And standing next to the shotgun were two rifles with big scopes on them. There were two shelves at the back of the safe full of ammunition for the guns. At the bottom of the safe there was a large bag. I pulled this out first and opened it on the floor. There were a couple of tools in it. I had no idea what they were for – more to research. I left them in and added to them the three large guns. I also set the bloody gun in it as well. I kept the clean gun in my hand and shoved all the boxes of shells into the bag.

Holy shit *that* bag was heavy. Good thing the adrenaline hadn't fully subsided from my system. I lugged it over to the hole in the bedroom wall and peered into my bedroom. First, I saw the bloody mess of the boy and then Jess sitting on my mattress with her face in her hands. She was crying.

"Jess, you ok?" I knew it was a stupid question as soon as it came out of my mouth. When she raised her head out of her hands and glared at me, I knew not to ask that question again.

"Steve, I'm not going to answer that one. I can't stay here tonight. I don't feel safe here anymore." The tears streamed down her face, but there was a hardness that overshadowed the tear-streaked exterior. "Steve, we have to go today. I don't care where, but we have to go."

"My thoughts exactly. It isn't going to be fun or easy, but I agree completely! Here." I struggled to get the duffle bag through the hole in the wall. Do you think you can drag this over to where the other ones are? We are at least armed now."

Her face hardened further. "What did you find?"

"Guns! I don't know what they all are, but I think I can figure out how to use them." I looked at her apologetically, "I've never held a gun before. I am going to look for more supplies now. Ten, fifteen minutes tops and we can start figuring out how to get out of here." I gave her a smile.

She got off the bed and came over to the hole, put her hands on both sides of it, leaned in and to my amazement, planted a kiss on my mouth. I barely had time to respond when she pulled away, reaching down to grab the bag and begin half dragging and half carrying it back across the room toward the living room. Not a word. But my spirits soared.

I crouched there for a second to watch her walk from the room and admire her ass as she went. I'm still a guy, no matter what is going on around me, right? My cloud of lust vaporized when I turned and saw the room around me.

I walked back to the closet. I wasn't interested in the clothes so shoved them to the side as best I could. There was another duffle bag on the floor. I grabbed it and opened it. Empty. Damn! I'm not sure what I was hoping for, but aside from the little monster almost eating my face, it was turning into my lucky day. I looked for a couple more seconds and found nothing else of interest in the closet. I surveyed the room again.

I had to get out of there. The blood and stench was too much. That room was a real buzz-kill. Through the hole in the wall I could hear Jess shuffling the duffle bag full of guns. The sound was way too loud for my comfort. I didn't have time to marvel at how sound is relative. Not at that moment, at least. Now I do. When silence is absolute, it is amazing how loud every little sound is amplified.

I walked to the bedroom door that was ajar and opened it with my foot. I had the gun raised and ready for anything. There was nothing there, just the living room. It appeared that their apartment was the mirror image of my own. That helped. I went straight to their pantry and found a ton of canned goods. Too heavy. We already had five heavy bags. There were a few food items that I had to take. Mostly comfort food like a package of Nestle Tollhouse Chewy Chocolate Chip Cookies. Those will be awesome later. Into the bag. Peanut butter, check – into the bag. Unopened grape jelly – into the bag. Saltines – into the bag since we had no bread. There were a couple other things that I tossed in as well, but we had enough food essentials to last us awhile.

As I walked through the living room, a sound stopped me in my tracks and sent a shiver of ice through my veins. The front doorknob jiggled. *Fuck, please be locked. Please be locked. Please be locked.* I stood at the top of the stairs looking down at the handle moving. The door didn't open. That was encouraging. I hoped it was not opening because it was locked and not because they were unable to fully turn the handle. Looking back, I probably should have gone down there to double check.

Encouraged yet scared into action I went on to the second bedroom. That was the kid's room. I skipped that one and walked into the bedroom at the end of the hall. Phil's office was immaculate. He probably didn't allow Patty or the boy in there at all, and I could imagine him threatening them with a beating if they touched anything in that room. There was a computer desk, like any that sits in a million home offices around the nation. There was a monitor on top and a place for the PC to the left of where he would have sat. There wasn't a single piece of paper on the desk.

There were maps on the wall: the US, a world map, and a map of Europe. There were pushpins all over these. There were pictures of Patty and Cameron – that's the boy's name – on the wall above the desk. I wondered if he put them up there or if Patty had done it to remind him that he had a family. He struck me as the type of guy that completely neglects his family. The type who feels that bringing home a paycheck and keeping the family fed, clothed and housed is enough family duty for him.

There wasn't much else in this room, so I went to the closet. I opened it and found an anally organized wall of shelves. The shelves had computer parts and tools on them. I saw a few items I had to have. I tossed in four rolls of duct tape, two cans of WD-40 and a riot helmet. That would definitely be handy. And it made me think of something else to look for in their closest.

As I was stuffing the helmet into the bag, I heard a noise behind me. I stood and whirled and pulled the trigger on the gun all at once. All that happened was an empty click. And thank god! Standing in front of me was Jessica.

"Fuck!" I exclaimed and threw my arms around her, "I'm so sorry. You scared the shit out of me."

"I'm sorry, I couldn't be alone any more. You could have killed me." Her voice was quavering with fear and anger all at once.

"Thank god it isn't loaded."

She pulled back from me and slapped me square in the face. "That's for almost killing me. We aren't even anymore. You owe me now big time."

"Yes. I am done in here now. Let's go figure out how to get out of here." I put my hand on my cheek and felt the heat from the slap on my hand. I also felt the sting of it all the way to my teeth. This girl packs a wallop.

"I wanted to tell you, there are more of them out there now. I don't know if they heard us or what, but there are about fifteen or twenty of them trying to get into our apartment, as well as the downstairs neighbor's. They are already in down below here. The door was open I guess. What are we going to do?" Her eyes were pleading with me for an answer.

"Let's go have a look. I'm sure we can figure something out." I said it, but I wasn't sure of anything anymore. I almost killed this girl. I followed her out of the room and through the living room, stopping to look down the stairs where the doorknob rattled more earnestly. Or maybe that was just my imagination. Who knows?

Into the bloody bedroom we went. I followed her through the hole in the wall that led to my (our? Did she say our?) apartment.

"Wait a second, there's one more thing I need to check for." I popped back into the bedroom, ran to the closet and grabbed what I had hoped to find, and almost ran back through the hole in the wall.

When I got through the wall, I held out the flak jacket to Jess.

We now have six bags on the stairs by the front door. I have prioritized them mentally, and now we are getting ready to get the fuck outta Dodge.

I just changed my status from "Available for chat" to "Jake, read my blog, we'll be there before dark with any luck at all."

Tuesday, September 18, 2012   7pm (hand written into a spiral notebook)

Holy shit, it's been a decade or more since I have written my blog (used to call it a journal) by hand. Not sure I can do this. My pencil can't keep up with my thoughts. But I have to try. What an incredible eight hours! I can barely believe we made it out of San Antonio alive. It was close a couple of times. Getting out of the apartment was fucking insane. Here is where this gets really geeky, but I think it kept me alive trying to escape the apartment.

I changed into a long sleeve turtleneck and commenced with the duct tape. I began wrapping the shirt in the silver tape until the entire shirt was covered, from wrist to neck and neck to waist. My logic was that there was no way they could bite through duct tape. I made sure not to wrap it too tight, however. I didn't want my movement restricted. And I wanted to be able to take it off and put it back on as needed. I completely taped a pair of sweat pants as well.

After I made the duct tape suit for myself (with a little help from Jess when it was impossible for me to reach certain spots), I helped Jess into the flak jacket. She had no hesitation or embarrassment to strip down to her bra and thong panties. I must admit right here and now, it was agony. Her skin is so soft, and that is after a few days of showers with only my men's soaps and products. I can imagine how she feels when she is using her girlie stuff. I digress. I helped her into the flak jacket and another of my turtlenecks, and commenced duct taping her as well. I did the same with another pair of my sweats. I won't get sidetracked with a description of the lower half of her body, but rest assured it is burned into my brain like a fine painting that would have made Leonardo da Vinci proud.

I found a couple pairs of leather gloves that we could use as well. I surveyed Jess in her full "zombie battle armor" and realized that the chivalry must not be completely dead in me. I noticed that she was covered from head to toe. I however would be exposed from the mid-neck on up. Jessica looked like an alien invader. Hopefully, if we run into anyone else, they won't be as afraid of aliens as they are of zombies.

When we were all decked out in our zombie battle armor, we surveyed outside again. Not good. There were still about 20 shamblors within view. Most had given up trying to get into the apartments. That was one good thing. I was hoping that would be the case. I was worried about getting the bags into the car. I prioritized them. The first trip I was going to get the guns into the back and she was going to throw the camping bag in. If it looked like we could make another trip we were going to get the rest of the bags in a second trip. But only if it looked like we could do it safely.

While we were making the suits, we discussed the plan to get out of there. Now we were ready for action. Jessica took up her place at my window and peered through the blinds and I started to walk toward my bedroom.

"Steve?" I turned and Jess was right in front of me, she dropped the helmet on the floor, she threw her arms around me and kissed me deeply. "Be careful, I'll do my part, you be careful with your part and hurry safe."

"Hurry safe?" But her lips crushed the question away. Then she pulled away and walked back to the window.

If that wasn't motivation to succeed, I don't know what is. I turned and walked into my bedroom. I stepped over Cameron and to the hole in the wall. I stepped through it with only the handgun on me, now fully loaded and safety released. I emerged into the neighbor's bedroom like a silver cat burglar. Everything was as it had been a couple hours before. I went through the bedroom door and into the living room. The knot of fear in my stomach tightened with each step I took toward the top of the stairs. My courage was hanging by a thread at that moment, and probably would have snapped if I had heard the doorknob move.

That didn't happen though and everything moved ahead almost as planned. I got to the top of the steps and peered down at the front door. My stomach clenched, wanting to wretch again. The feeling passed and I took the first step down before the terror could try to sabotage me. I reached the bottom of the stairs and looked out the peephole. There were only three of them in the line of sight of the fish eye. That worked for me, especially since the closest one was about ten feet away, and all three were facing the other direction, one of these was actually at my front door, pawing at the doorknob. I reached for the blinds that covered the window on the wall to the right of the door. I took a deep breath and pulled the drawstring all the way down. The blinds shot up and I opened the front door all the way against the wall. I wrapped the string around the doorknob as quickly as I could while I watched in slow motion as the three zombies I saw from the peephole and four others that I hadn't seen all turned toward me at the sound of the door opening.

As I wrapped the cord around the doorknob I stole a glance up at my living room window. There was a gap in the closed blinds and I could clearly see Jessica's face staring down at me. She looked as terrified as I felt. My eyes went back to the zombies and it was time to retreat. The closest was shambling toward me. Ten feet can be erased really fast, even with their awkward stiff legged shamble. He was only a step from the doorway. If I had stuck my arm out I could have grabbed his outstretched hands. I turned and ran up the stairs.

I should say I tried to run up the stairs; I ran up one step and then tripped. *That* was *not* part of the plan! I tripped on the second carpeted step and slid down to the floor again. I turned and looked at the zombie looking down at me and scrambled up the steps on my hands and knees. I almost made it out of reach. I felt the hand clamp around my ankle and looked down between my arms and legs in time to see it bite into my silvery calf. The pain was excruciating. I kicked out with my other foot and it flew back against the tied-open door. I saw another of them step through the door and head straight toward me, completely ignoring the one I just kicked. This time I scrambled out of reach and up to the top of the stairs in a flash.

When I got to the top, I looked back down the stairs. If the pain in my leg hadn't been so blinding, the sight of three zombies trying to climb stairs would have been extremely comical. They were tripping over each other, falling down and making absolutely no progress.

I limped to the bedroom, closed and locked the door. I stood with my back against it for a second before calling out, "Jess, come help me, please."

She had apparently been right on the other side of the wall, because before I finished my request she jumped through the hole in the wall.

"Are you ok? What happened?" She was near panic.

"I think I'm ok. One of them bit my leg, but I don't think they got through the tape. Those fuckers are *strong!* How can they possibly be so strong? Fuck, how can they even *be*? Help me get this dresser in front of the door."

We moved the enormous twelve-drawer dresser in front of the door. While we were shoving it in place, I wondered how the hell they got it in here in the first place. After it was in place, we went through the hole again.

"Get on the bed," Jess told me sternly as soon as we were both through the wall.

"Huh?" I uttered, bewildered.

"I'm going to check your leg."

"Ah," and I lay on my stomach on the bed and felt her raise my duct taped pants leg. I heard the sharp intake of breath when she looked at the injury, and then I felt her fingers on my leg. Finally, I heard her sigh. It was clearly the sigh of relief from someone who had been holding their breath.

"It didn't break the skin. You are going to have one fuck of a bruise and it's going to hurt for a while, but you'll be fine. You're a genius with your duct tape idea. Can you walk on it enough to get us the fuck out of here now? Now that we've let them in over there, it is only a matter of time before they get in here." She looked at me, her eyes pleading with me to be ok.

I wasn't lying to her when I said, "Yeah, I'll be fine, let's get the fuck out of here. Let's see if they are all going in."

We both went to the living room window and looked out. Of the twenty that were out there earlier, we could only see three. One was just inside the neighbor's front door. The other two were hot on his heels. If you could call how they moved "hot."

While we watched, the one inside the door stumbled and bumped into the door. It continued up the steps and out of sight. The cord on the door came completely undone and the door slammed shut. That complicated things slightly. But two was better than twenty.

Jessica must have thought the same thing. "We can outrun two of them right? Look how slow they are?"

"No sweat, hun. I think we will even have time to get all the bags. It will take them awhile to cover the sixty feet from that door to ours. And if we are off and running before they even hear the sound of the door opening, we'll have no problem at all."

So we went for it. I got my keys in hand and we went down the stairs to the front door. I removed the boards bracing the door. I took one last look out the peephole and saw both of the zombies pawing at the neighbor's front door. I reached down, picked up the gun bag and hefted it over my shoulder. Jessica had the backpack over her shoulder and a smaller bag of clothes in her hand.

I flung the door open…

I ran-limped headlong out the front door. I hit the key-fob twice to unlock all the doors to the SUV. I ran around the front of the car, down the driver's side to the back, flung open the cargo hatch and tossed in the bag. Jess was right there to toss in her bags. The two zombies that had turned around from the neighbor's front door were shambling toward us. There was plenty of time to grab the rest of the bags. I ran back (the adrenaline was quickly easing the pain in my leg) to the apartment door and grabbed three more bags. As I turned to bolt for the car again, I ran into Jess. We jostled momentarily and I turned sideways so she could grab the last two bags sitting on the stairs. When we turned around to go back to the car there was a zombie walking toward us. It came out from behind Xena.

Dropping the bags, I raised the handgun, pointed it at the zombie's face and pulled the trigger. I watched a small hole appear in its nose and the back of its head blow out. It fell in a crumpled heap to the ground. I stepped over it and moved to the cargo door and tossed in the bags. Jess did the same and we slammed the door down. We opened the front doors and jumped in at the same time. I jammed the key into the ignition, fired Xena to life, jammed it into reverse and hit the gas.

There was a big thud and a scraping sound under the car. I didn't care. It was time to get the fuck out! I was turned around looking behind me after that. I didn't want to hit a car or something that might incapacitate Xena. And we weren't even close to alone.

My heart lurched when I got beyond the cover of the building. There were perhaps a hundred of them walking towards us. I guess the sound of the car had drawn them away from whatever they were trying to get at. They were in all different states of gore. Some were completely covered in blood and some were completely clean. They were also in all states of dress and undress. The vast majority of them were in nightclothes. Most of them must have died in bed.

I hit a couple more while I was in reverse and turned them into speed bumps. We bounced down the curb into the parking lot and I threw the car into drive and headed for the closed gate. *They* were closing in all around us. I reached for the key fob as I approached the gate. The gate had about twenty more zombies reaching through it trying to get in. There is no way we would have gotten out of there if we had waited for the power to go out. The gate started to roll open and then stopped after about three feet.

"Fuck-a-doodle-do," I exclaimed, seeing that there were feet and limbs under the wheels of the gate. A fucking safety feature threatened to cause our death. "No!" I screamed as I saw the gate start to reverse direction. There was no time to think about the consequences. There were zombies at all the car windows inside the gate, there were two dozen on the other side of the gate causing the gate to close. I then heard a fist on the window to my left. I am man enough to admit that I screamed like a little girl at the sound and looked into the face of the apartment manager.

'Hang on Jess!' I stamped on the accelerator and Xena lurched forward into the gate, inches before it latched shut. The zombie disappeared from my peripheral vision and the gate sprung open off its track to the right. And then it caught on the front of Xena. "Shit!," I yelled as we started dragging the gate with us, zombies holding onto it. The fuckers were still trying to get at us. Relentless bastards! I got to the end of the driveway and when it was obvious the gate wasn't going to fall off on its own, I hit the break. It wavered, but held. I threw the gear shifter into reverse again and slammed the gas all the way to the floor. Success. The gate fell forward off the car.

I hit the brake and we were again inside the complex. I glanced in the rear view mirror and gawked at what I saw. I couldn't believe it. There were two figures running toward us from about a hundred yards behind us. They had what looked like bats in their hands and they were swinging at any zombies that were near them as they ran.

There was no way they were going to make it to us. I only had a second to think, and the words went through my head: *'No chivalry? You can't leave them.'*

"Fuck me," I uttered under my breath as I hit the gas again. Xena again responded by lurching backwards through the crowding walking dead, sending some of them under and others bouncing off to the sides.

"The fuck are you doing? Drive!" And she looked back and saw what I had seen. "Hurry, they aren't going to make it," she encouraged me on.

We met them about 75 yards back and they yanked on the handles on both rear doors. Locked. I fumbled and unlocked the doors. The rear passenger door opened immediately and a woman threw herself in and slammed the door shut behind her. Behind my door, a man had turned from my car and was swinging at one of the zombies that had gotten too close for comfort. His aim wasn't true and he hit it in the shoulder. It kept coming at him. It got a hand on his arm and he was unable to swing again. I saw him shove it back with the bat, one hand at each end. It staggered back two steps, which gave him just enough time to fling open the door and dive in. I hit the gas and Xena lurched backwards.

"Shit!" I exclaimed and slammed on the brakes. The door swung closed behind me. Well, it would have closed if his legs hadn't been still hanging out. He let out a scream of shock and pain. He scrambled the rest of the way in as I shifted back into drive. The woman was yanking him in by the belt. "You in?"

They both shouted back at me as one, "Yes, go!"

Once again I stamped on the gas. We flew forward through the zombies that were thick ahead and to either side of us now. It wasn't easy to keep control of the car but somehow I drove on instinct and managed to fly out the gate and to the street. I slowed only enough to keep from toppling the whole car on its side. My passengers in the back were thrown into the driver's side door but they remained inside.

Once on the road outside the complex I headed toward I-10, which with any luck would take us to Houston by dinnertime. Did I say luck? Yeah, it wasn't meant to be.

***

The two in the back untangled themselves and put their seatbelts on. I kept an eye on them in the rear view mirror while they situated themselves. Jess turned around in her seat and initiated conversation.

"'Hi, I'm Jessica and this is Stephen. We're headed to Houston to meet up with some friends of Stephen's. He's been talking to them since all this started and Stephen and his friend seem to have a plan of sorts. What plan do you guys have?" Jess smiled her big beautiful bartender smile and I could see some of the tension in our new guests melt away. Under the circumstances, any tension break was a great thing.

The woman spoke first. She was not as feminine as Jess. She had short mousy brown hair. She spoke with very thin lips and forced a smile back to Jess that looked like a grimace. "We're Tammy and Paul Roberts. Thank you for coming back for us. I'm sorry to put you at risk, but we were desperate and scared and when we heard the car after seeing *them* walking away toward the front of the complex, we had to take the chance. Thank you both so very much for coming back for us." She burst into tears after spilling this barrage of a greeting and apology. It was all run together in one breath as if it were one sentence. Her gratitude, fear and relief gushed out of her in a wave. She fell sideways into Paul's lap and began to sob loudly.

"Nice to meet you, Paul and Tammy. I'd shake your hands if I weren't driving. I've been afraid that there weren't many people left. But if there are at least four of us in one complex, then the chances of there being others are pretty good." I smiled into the mirror at Paul.

"Thank you. You are," he paused, "*We* are headed to Houston are we? Tell me what the plan is then."

"I've got a friend and his family that live there…"

"How do you know they are still alive? And how could you talk to them? The phones are all down. Our cells don't work, and our land line has been down since Saturday." he interrupted.

"I've been chatting with him online every day for the past few days, including earlier this morning. I don't know what the plan will be when we get there, but I've known him since we were about eight years old and we've talked and planned for this apocalypse since we were kids. I know that sounds pretty stupid, but he is someone I definitely want by my side during this event."

"Stephen, that is exactly the sort of thing I would have laughed at a week ago. I have students - I taught philosophy at UTSA - who talked about the 'Zombie Apocalypse' as if it were an eventuality. They were right, but I always thought they were wasting such important time in their life, better utilized in otherwise productive activities. Brainy was apparently wrong. Brainy is what Tammy calls me. I am in your debt and at your service Stephen. Onward to Houston." He flashed me a genuine, huge grin, as if he were a child embarking on an adventure. The child-like grin belied the outward appearance. Paul looked every bit the stereotypical college philosophy teacher. He wore spectacles and a sweater (I don't get that. It's hot as hell here in San Antonio in September.) His hair looked like someone had put a brown mop on top of his head and the greying goatee he was sporting conveyed a definite sense of laid-backness.

"That's it?" I asked. "You aren't going to try to rationalize this whole thing and make our lives miserable trying to explain how none of this is possible? That is what happens in the movies. There is always a Doubting Thomas. He is usually one of the first to die, of course, but there is always one." I gave him my best evil grin in the mirror.

He laughed heartily. "That's exactly why I am *not* going to be the Doubting Thomas of the group. I am just going to be the loving husband and good helper in any way I can. I've always wanted to live to a ripe old age. That desire hasn't changed in the last few days." He looked down at his wife and stroked her hair as her sobs subsided. "How long have you two been together?"

I looked at Jess and decided to let her field that question. That way I would get my answer to whether or not we were actually together.

Jess grinned when she saw the look on my face. Apparently, I can be read like a book. "He's the man I've looked for my whole life, and it took the zombie apocalypse to weed out the loser bullshitheads for me to recognize what I really wanted in life. So in answer to your question, we've been together since he charged into my apartment and saved me from a hungry hoard of undead trying to eat my brains. When was that honey? Two nights ago? Seems like forever."

I think I actually blushed as she was telling our new traveling mates this.

"Well there it is then. I've had a girlfriend for two days now and I didn't even know it. Maybe I should have taken advantage of you in your sleep then." I'm sure I was grinning like an idiot as I said this. I know I wasn't watching the road. I watched Jessica laugh, puckered and blew me a kiss. Then her face turned to horror and she screamed.

"Watch out Stephen!" She braced herself by putting her hands on the dashboard.

I turned forward just in time to feel the impact and see the zombie hit my fender, bounce up onto the hood, and onto the windshield, cracking the shit out of it before flying up over Xena. I even saw it fall to the pavement behind us in the rearview mirror.

"Fuck!" I exhaled and replaced my hands on the wheel at ten and two o'clock. I sat up straight and focused all my concentration ahead of us. *They* were coming out toward the road from both sides, drawn by the sound of a motorized vehicle. Now I wish I had one of those quiet hybrids, though I couldn't see a Prius bowling over even one of these fuckers.

My new romance erased from my mind as I was slammed back into the realization of the mortal danger we were in. Our lives hung in the balance because we were air breathers. There wasn't a sign of other survivors on the road. I hoped to run into someone. Anyone would have been great. But as far as I could tell, we were the only four people left alive in San Antonio. Hell, it may be the four of us and the four of you in Houston, Jake. We'll find out.

This was nothing like how the movies portray it. Maybe because of the way it all came about. So many people died in their homes. I swerved to miss the zombies far more often than I swerved to avoid stalled or parked cars.

I merged onto I-10 going east. There were no cars and no more zombies to avoid. I was beginning to get optimistic that we would get into Houston by mid-afternoon. Thinking that apparently jinxed us. About a mile after getting on the freeway, we saw the first of the zombies. I should have gotten off the freeway right away. First, there was just one of them. I was puzzled about how it had gotten on the freeway when there were still no cars in sight. Then I thought it could have stumbled miles in the days since this shit started.

It turns out it had wandered quite far. But it hadn't wandered *onto* the freeway as I had surmised. It was probably wandering back from its vehicle. It was quite bloodied and mangled, a man in a business suit. One arm was completely gone and the other torn partially from its socket and hanging limp at its side as it walked toward us. It looked like a very unbalanced game of chicken. A game which amazingly the zombie won. I didn't want to damage our transportation any more than I already had. I swerved at the last second and drove to the right of the zombie. I watched it in the rear view mirror as it turned and started walking back the way it had come – following us in the Eastbound lanes of I-10.

The further we got the more zombies we encountered. We saw a few cars stalled. Some of them had their doors flung wide open and some did not. All of the ones we passed that were closed contained at least one zombie. Some were feasting on their unfortunate traveling partners, while others tried in vain to get through the car windows and out into the world where they could feast on the living – assuming we aren't the last ones left.

The closer we got to the edge of town, the more cars we passed. There were less that looked like stalls, and more that were accidents. Just like with the stalls behind us, any vehicle completely closed had zombies. I was relieved that there weren't that many open, thus not a huge amount of zombies on the freeway. I had to slow way down in order to get by accidents that took up all lanes and forced us to the shoulder to pass.

Then we got to a place where the road was completely impassable.

There had been a massive pileup. It was as if car after car had slammed into the vehicular wall ahead of us now. I couldn't tell how far the blockage was because there was a curve in the freeway just ahead of us. At the sound of Xena, several zombies started to appear from over the wreckages and move toward us. First falling from the vehicles, then getting up and shambling forward. I turned Xena around as quickly as I could and started to head west on the eastbound side. Where was a cop when you needed one? I would have gladly accepted a ticket for this. Alas, I had to backtrack to the next onramp. Every zombie I had passed going east was in the way going west. I slowed down for each one and tried to avoid them. The ones I couldn't avoid, I did my best to hit with one of the corners of my hood so they would deflect to the side rather than onto the hood and possibly into our laps.

I got off the freeway and tried to take the access road east along the freeway. But the access road was just as congested. We had to weave in and out of city streets, and accumulated a crowd of zombies in our wake everywhere we went. I was the Pied-Fucking-Piper of zombies.

This circuitous route cost us a lot of time and we decided to try to leave the city via non-freeway roads. This was the best idea of the day because I had also misremembered how much gas I had in Xena. By the time we decided to change routes, I was down to about half a tank. That most definitely would not get us to Jake's house.

***

I drove north from I-10 to a road that ran northeast, away from the center of the city. It didn't take long to get out of the city once we got away from the highway. We had to keep moving at a decent pace to keep the zombies approaching from the sides from cutting us off. I clipped a few of them as I steered us out of the city. There was blessed little vehicular congestion on this road once we passed the sign that said we were leaving San Antonio. The only congestion we saw consisted of cars in various stages of rust parked in front of old farmhouses. I gauged we would have to be on this road for about thirty to forty miles before it would be safe to cut south to I-10 for a second attempt at the eastbound part of the journey. I kept a close eye on the fuel indicator and felt panic when it dipped below a quarter tank, but we shortly came to a service station and I pulled in.

"Ok guys, I need to stop for gas. I would feel much better about it if you all would get out and watch for *them* while I fill her up. Would you do that for me?"

"Yes, Stephen," Jess said with a very "duh" attitude in her voice and look on her face.

"Yeah," Tammy said matter-of-factly.

"Of course, Stephen," Paul said with great enthusiasm.

I pulled into the station. It appeared to be empty, but who the fuck knows these days. I jumped out and almost ran into the rear door as it opened and Paul got out in a hurry to be of assistance. I also heard the other two doors open as the girls got out of the passenger side. I noticed that all three carried baseball bats. *It's good to be the hero. I have my own vigilante baseball bat wielding gang,* I thought and chuckled to myself.

I pulled the nozzle off the gas pump, unscrewed my gas cap, inserted the nozzle and squeezed the trigger. Nothing happened. I stared at the pump in disbelief. How can this be happening? Then I realized the problem and let out a guffaw, quickly stifled it and looked around.

"I have to pay for the gas. Thank goodness these things are automated. Probably the last thing I will be paying for, at least for the foreseeable future." I let out a snort of laughter this time. I heard a giggle from Jess and nothing from Tammy. Paul grinned nervously as I reached into my pocket for my wallet. I pulled it out, extracted my debit card and slid it into the slot. I punched in a few digits. "If anyone cares to know, my PIN number to my debit card is 4827," I started laughing. I couldn't help it. I was controlling my volume as best I could but I couldn't stop the laughter as I was pumping the gas. I couldn't stop, that is, until the power in the service station cut out.

"What the fuck? No, no no," I said and then let out a sigh. Not a sigh of relief but one to calm myself. This was something out of my control; I needed to adjust to the new circumstance. I looked at the gallons I had pumped and the numbers read 15.679. Not quite full, but pretty damn close. It would be more than enough to get us to Houston under normal circumstances. Normal was the farthest from our current circumstance, however.

"Who wants to go shopping? It's all on me." I waved my debit card in the air indicating my method of payment and began to giggle quietly again. "Let's get what we can while we're here. It appears to be deserted."

Paul chimed in then. "We don't want to deplete your supplies. But let's be very careful about this. Let's make sure there is no one or thing inside before we let our guard down and shop. Someone should keep watch just inside the door to make sure none of them come from out here."

"Absolutely," I agreed. We all walked up to the front door, baseball bats in hand. I peered through the glass of the door as I reached for the handle. After not seeing anything, I turned to my crew and asked, "Ready? The less noise we make the better. Sounds seem to draw them, so let's get in and out as quick as we can. Who knows how many heard us drive in here. Jess would you stand guard inside the door and keep an eye out here, please? Let us know if you see any of them."

They all nodded, I pulled on the handle and it opened. Apparently, there was no time to lock up. That set me on high alert right away. Not locked could mean there were some of them in there. I took a deep breath and stepped inside. The others followed right behind me. I went behind the counter to check for an undead clerk and found none. I grabbed several cheap plastic bags.

As I handed one to Jess, I said, "Let us know if you see anything. Grab what you can by the door." I leaned down slightly and planted a quick kiss on her mouth. She kissed me back. As I pulled away, her hand went to the back of my head and her kiss became more passionate, her lips parting. I took this as an invitation and my tongue found hers. After a moment that felt like a lifetime, we parted.

"Please be careful Stephen. I want to get out of here and back on the road." Her eyes were a mixture of desire and pleading.

"I will, sweetheart. I want more of that," indicating her lips as I leaned down and kissed her quickly again.

I turned and saw Tammy and Paul watching with big grins on their faces. I characteristically blushed as I handed them each bags.

"Ok, let's check out here and then we can go in the back office together to make sure there are none in there," I said.

"No, we don't need to go back there for anything"' Paul said. "Everything we might need will be out here. Stephen, would you grab all the medical stuff? I know it's mostly just aspirin and stuff, but I'd feel a little better having it all."

"You got it. Let's check the aisles first. Make sure there are none of them in here. I'm sure they would have been on us already, but let's check just to make sure. Caution will be key from now on."

The store wasn't very big. Only three aisles. One had the candy and chips. Another had the overpriced household goods, including the pain meds. The last, which was opposite the four coolers full of water, beer, sodas and energy drinks, had the grocery items. Your typical Anywhere, USA gas station convenience store.

Reconnaissance complete without incident, we started the task of filling our bags. I filled one of mine with all the Advil, Tylenol, Xantac (who knows?) Pepto Bismol, and everything remotely pharmaceutical that I saw. This included band-aids and Neosporin. I grabbed a bag full of canned goods as well. There wasn't much to choose from. A few soups and beans were all that was available, but it all went into a bag.

"Paul, would you grab as much water as you can. That's even more important than the food," I said barely above a whisper. All of a sudden, I had a fear of being there. I couldn't explain it, but there was a growing feeling of unease in the pit of my stomach.

"On it," he replied in the same hushed tone. I noticed his face was pale. The same dread seemed to have also come over him.

Tammy was by his side, silently grabbing loaves of bread and other perishables by the coolers.

I stole a glance over at Jessica and she was standing at the door with a full bag in her hands. She was trying to look everywhere at once and obviously nervous. *Oh god, what's coming? Why are we all so jittery all of a sudden?*

I had three bags full from the aisle I was in and moved over to the aisle where the other two were. I opened the cooler with the energy drinks – FDA warnings be damned – and filled my bag with these as Paul was in the cooler filling bag after bag with water.

Tammy had four full bags and was standing watching. She was done shopping and took to looking around nervously.

I turned back to my cooler, reaching for another can of Monster and then saw it. Two eyes looking back at me from the gloom behind the cans. Then the hands reached through and tried to grab my hand. The fingers grazed the back of my hand as I yanked it back. It didn't make a sound. No moaning like in the movies. More like a silent predator trying not to give away its location and intentions.

"Fuck," I gasped. "Let's get out of here. You guys ready? I've seen enough. Let's quit while we're ahead." I started walking toward the front door and saw Jess staring at me. She was stiff as a board.

"There's one out there. Across the street. It just came out of the trees over there. It's all bloody. Let's get out of here," she pleaded.

"Seconded, motion carried. Unanimous? Yeah? Let's go." Paul whispered.

We all walked toward the front door. The only sound was our footsteps and the zombie in the back trying to get through the cans in the cooler into the main part of the store. The bags were in our hands and the baseball bats under our arms. Not the most defensive arrangement, but out of necessity it was the way it had to be. Only Jess had her bat in hand. She pushed the door open and walked out, holding the door for us. Her eyes riveted on the zombie walking toward us. It had just passed beyond the painted line in the middle of the street. We had plenty of time to get to the car and get the fuck out.

We hurried to Xena, I opened the rear hatch and tossed my bags in. The baseball bat fell from under my arm and rolled under the car.

"Shit," I hissed, and dropped to my hands and knees to reach for my weapon.

Paul had the same issue I did because I heard the loud clang of his bat also hit the pavement. It startled me and I jerked in surprise. My head connected with the underside of the car and I briefly saw stars.

"Jessica! Behind you!" Tammy whisper-yelled.

That brought me back from my stun in a hurry. My hand closed on the barrel of my bat. I began to pull it out and wiggle out from under the car. I heard a bag hit the ground. As I got to my feet, I saw Jess with a bat in both hands, spinning in place swinging for the fences. Only her target wasn't a baseball, it was the head of a child that had shambled up behind us. And the child wasn't alone. There were three others coming from around the side of the gas station.

Jessica connected squarely on the side of the kid-zombie's head and it fell to the ground. It hit the pavement and immediately reached for her feet. Then I heard more bags hit the ground and Tammy was right there bringing her bat down on the skull of the kid like a war hammer in a medieval battle. There was a sickening crunch and what was once a skull was now a caved in mass of hair, bone and grey matter.

The three behind the boy were still about twenty yards away but getting closer one shambling step at a time. I turned back to the zombie across the street. It wasn't across the street anymore. It was only about twenty feet away.

"Get the stuff in the car and get in." I said and walked the distance between me and the zombie. As I was readying the bat for my walking swing, its face became a snarl, and then it opened its mouth and raised its arms toward me. I swung with all my might and connected. I missed its head though. I heard the same bone crunching sound and one of its arms fell to its side. It kept advancing without even noticing its useless arm. I pulled the bat back for another swing. I took one step back and then stepped into my second swing. This time I connected for a grand slam. I struck it square in the ear and watched as its face squashed to the left. Then it crumpled to the ground in a heap.

I spun to see my three companions picking up the dropped bags and goods from the ground and throwing them into the car. Tammy slammed the hatch shut and they ran to their doors. They jumped in the car and I heard three doors slam simultaneously. The three zombies had halved their distance to us at this point and I didn't wait any longer to survey the situation. It was time to flee. I covered the twenty feet to the driver's door in five running steps, bloody bat at my side.

I jumped in, fired the car to life and sped out of the gas station. As I drove away, I looked in the rearview and saw something that made me hit the brakes. I gawked in the mirror not believing what I was seeing. The three zombies were bending over the dead boy tearing and biting chunks of flesh from the child's corpse.

"What are you doing?" Jess asked in an adrenaline fueled panic tone.

"They're eating him. Look!" I exclaimed.

Everyone turned and gawked out the back of the car. Various surprised sounds issued from each of them. We were riveted by the scene behind us, until we heard something hit the hood ahead of us. We turned in our seats as one. There were two more of them.

"Enough already," I said as I hit the gas. One of them disappeared underneath the car and the other was flung to the side and spun around, but was still standing. I drove east again. After a few minutes of uneventful driving, I started the conversation.

"Ok, you all saw that right? They were eating one of their own, right? That wasn't a living child we killed was it?" I asked hoping for reassurance.

"No, it was definitely one of them." Tammy said. Tears streamed down her face. "Zombie or not, it was still a child. I know we had to, but it still hits me hard." She leaned into Paul's shoulder, he put his arm around her and she buried her head in his chest.

Paul said, "No, he was definitely one of them. If they eat each other, why don't they kill each other? Why do they come for the living? I don't get it." He stroked Tammy's hair and kissed the top of her head, "Shhhhhh, you had to do it. If you hadn't, he might have gotten one of us. We all have to do things we normally wouldn't from now on, I think," he comforted.

"I wonder if we hide out long enough if they will start to eat each other before they are dead-dead," Jess said. "Are we going to get to Houston before dark? It's already five o'clock. I don't want to be outside after dark."

"I agree. Let's find a place to hole up for the night," I said.

***

We drove on in silence for another half hour on the two-lane farm road. After, I turned south toward I-10 I said, "I'd really like to

72

find a place with electricity in the next fifteen minutes or so. Keep your eyes out for a place to stop."

It only took about ten minutes to find a place.

"There!" Jessica almost shouted. She was pointing to the right about a quarter mile ahead. "The front porch light is on!"

"Fantastic! Any objections?" We all looked as we approached the farmhouse. It was an old building. Faded with peeling brownish paint. It was two stories and creepy as hell. "Aside from its resemblance to The Night of the Living Dead farmhouse that is?" I added.

"No, that's my only objection. Open fields all around. No place outside for zombies to jump out of. It gets my vote," Paul said as Tammy raised her head from his chest for the first time since we left the gas station.

"It's kinda big. Who knows what's inside," Tammy said.

"With any luck there might be more survivors in there. Strength in numbers right? That seems to be the key to the enemy's success," I said. "If not, then we can clean house while it's still light out, and there is electricity."

"Okay," she said meekly.

I turned into the dirt driveway and drove up the front porch steps. There were several cars in the driveway. I paused for a moment before killing the engine and decided we may need a quick getaway. I pulled away from the steps and backed Xena all the way up to the front steps until my tow hitch hit the top step and I felt the crunch as it splintered the wood.

"Oops. We've landed," I said and I turned to look at everyone. Fear was on everyone's faces. "We could stay in the car, but I'd rather see what's inside. I feel like a pirate plundering as we go. Believe me, I am just as scared as the rest of you but I really think we need this. Maybe we can even get a good night's sleep."

"Let's do it. I don't want to spend the night in the car. And time's a-wastin," Paul said.

"Ok," Tammy said still meek.

"Do we have a plan?" Jess asked, looking right at me.

"Check the downstairs room by room," I said. "Stay together, check the upstairs, and then if there is a basement, either check it or block it. I'd rather check it as long as there is power, but if I get voted down, I can live with that."

"No, if we're going to spend the night in there we need to check every nook and cranny," Tammy said adamantly. I was glad to see she was coming back from being withdrawn.

"Done. Let's get this over with, then, so we can relax a little," I said.

We got out and were standing two on each side of the vehicle. We didn't have to wait long to discover the occupants of the house. The front door was slightly ajar and we stood at the bottom of the steps to the porch as we watched an arm emerge from the doorway. The arm was followed by a head, then a torso, and then the rest of the zombie. It was quite a theatrical entrance.

When the zombie fully emerged, it faced us and paused for a moment. It was as if it couldn't decide which way to go. Soon, however, it took its first stumbling steps toward Paul and me.

"You ready, Paul?" I asked and then moved to the side of the steps. You stay there and I'll brain him when he gets to the bottom of the steps."

At least that was the plan. But as the old saying goes, "the best laid plans of mice and men…" It got to the top step and stepped off. Its undead body didn't compensate for the step down, and tumbled forward. It didn't flail. It didn't brace itself. It just fell forward into open space right at Paul. He wasn't ready for the sudden movement and neither was I. It flew right past me before I could swing. Paul couldn't swing before it was literally hitting him in the chest and knocking him backward to the ground. The thing's arms stayed in front of it the entire time it was airborne, and when it hit the ground on top of Paul, one arm landed straight into the dirt and snapped like a twig.

When Paul hit the ground flat on his back, I heard the wind explode out of him in an "Oof". His bat went flying behind him and he had one arm between him and the thing. He was writhing, trying to push it away from him. It was about to bite into his arm. I yanked it by the collar as hard as I could just as its teeth were about to sink into Paul's arm. I managed to pull it back, but not completely away from Paul as I hoped. Maybe if I had used two hands I would have succeeded, but I was holding the bat with the other hand. The zombie landed right next to Paul, its legs twisted up with his.

Paul tried to scramble back from it on his behind and hands, making slow progress because he was trying to catch his breath as well. The zombie now reached for me with its one good arm, gnashing its teeth on the air a foot from my ankle. It clamped its hand around my ankle with a vice-like grip. I could not pull away from it. I raised the bat above my head intending to bring it down on the thing's skull, but as I started my downward swing, a movement caught my eyes at the top of the steps. Another one had emerged and was making a straight line for me. It was already at the top step.

"Shit!" I yelled. "Jess, Tammy, help!"

But the thing at the top of the steps fell off. I had barely enough time to register that it was a big woman in a huge, bright yellow sundress. Before I could have a second thought, she was flying through the air like her husband (I assume that's what he used to be). I had just enough time to get the bat in front of me and push it at her with one end in each hand to try to deflect her. But she was three hundred pounds if she was an ounce and her full force was hurtling through the air at me. Before she hit me, I felt a sharp pain in my ankle and my eyes fell to the creature taking a bite out of me. Then the freight train hit me, a three hundred pound zombie with a baseball bat in her mouth (lucky placement on my part). She hit and I went down. I was looking at her massive neck when the bat hit me square in the forehead and everything went black.

***

When I came to, I was in the clutches of sheer terror. I could feel hard earth below me and someone shaking me gently.

"Fuck, fuck, fuck, help, get it off me!" I screamed.

"Easy, Stephen. Easy. It's me. It's Jessica. You're ok. They're dead. Sort of." Sure enough, it was Jess who was straddling me and gently shaking my shoulders. My eyes focused on hers and she smiled. She actually smiled at me.

"What the fuck happened? The big bitch landed on me and the old man bit my leg and now I'm waking up with you on top of me? What the fuck?!"

"Honey, slow down. They're done. We took care of them. Well, you put 'the big bitch' out of commission. Apparently, after the bat hit your forehead it bent her neck back so far her neck actually snapped. Don't ask me how. But she is over there. Tammy and I managed to roll her off you and a few feet away. The guy was *trying* to bite your ankle. But your zombie armor saved you again. You are going to have another huge bruise on your left ankle to match the one on your right calf. They can't move very fast, but these fuckers are strong.

"We got her off you and Tammy brained the man just as he was about to bite Paul, since the big one knocked you away from him. The zombies are both out of commission now. The woman is still gnashing her teeth, but it appears she can't move anything below her neck," She bent down and kissed my forehead and I winced with pain.

"Oh shit that hurts. How long have I been out?" I asked.

"Not long. A minute or two. Can you move everything?" she asked me and smiled when I was able to bring my arms up, put them behind her head and pull her down for a better kiss. This one was cut short by a wave of nausea and I had to turn my head from her and gag as the pain shot through my head like an ice pick. I didn't actually throw up, but it was close enough that Jess sat up and concern crossed her face.

When the wave of nausea passed and I turned back to Jess, she smiled again. I don't know how she can smile and just light me up inside, but it did this time. And not for the last time either.

"Ok hero. Here is the new plan. We are going to put you in the driver's seat and you are going to be the external lookout. We are going to go in and make sure the house is clear just like we originally planned. If you see anything move out here, you are going to lay on the horn. Think you can handle that? " she spoke this in a stern way that I knew meant no arguing. So I uttered the words that every man in a relationship needs to learn, know and accept from time to time.

"Yes dear," I said.

That only made her grin bigger. She bent down again and kissed me softly on the lips this time.

"Paul, will you help me get him in the car?"

"Of course. Is he going to be ok?" he asked her as if she were a doctor and I weren't laying right there in front of him.

I answered before she could, "I'm going to be sore in the morning, but I'll be just fine, man. Get me in the crow's nest while you three see what plunder there be inside this vessel, aarrgh," I said and squinted as I put a hand over one eye. But instead of getting a laugh like I hoped, I only got concerned looks from both of them. "I'm fine. Remember my comment about feeling like a pirate earlier?" I asked, working myself up on my elbows. My head swam for a moment and the world started to go grey. They were both at my side in a flash.

"Whoa, get me off this rollie coaster, mommy," I uttered before the world brightened to normal again. "Man, this sucks ass. I'm going to need some aspirin, and a shit-ton of it at that. Now get me in the car and check out the house."

They positioned themselves and got me to my feet slowly and carefully with very little jarring of my aching head. My legs were in pain as well. My right calf and left ankle felt like, well, like a zombie had been munching on them. Oh yeah, they had!

They walked me around Xena to the driver's seat and I was able to climb in. The effort left me light headed and they both stood there until the moment passed. I saw Paul turn around and Tammy was right by his side. I don't think they will be separable any time soon. I heard him ask if she was ok and if she was ready to go inside. Then I felt a breast brush against my arm. Granted it was through two layers of duct tape and three layers of clothing, but it was definitely a breast. Jessica was leaning into the cab in front of me. Her blue eyes stared into mine as if she were searching for something.

"What?" I asked.

"Why are you grinning?" she asked in return.

"Uh," I stammered a moment and then just had out with it, "I felt your booby." I felt my grin from ear to ear.

"Oh, really? Even through all this body armor?" she asked, returning my smile.

"Yeah, I'm like the Princess and the Pea who could feel the pea through thirty mattresses, only my power is with the boobies." I let out a laugh and winced as the ice pick jabbed behind my eyes again.

When I opened my eyes, the concern was back on her face. "Well, Mister Booby Man, you will have to feel a lot better before you get more than an accidental feel of them again. Got it?" she asked, but it was obviously a rhetorical question. So I waited for her to continue. "Your job right now is to watch out for us. If anything moves, you honk this horn. Got it?" This time I knew she wanted an answer.

"Yes Jessie. And your job is to be extra careful in there. I am going to have a hard time repopulating the world without you. You got that?" I asked and rested my hand on the back of her neck.

"I promise. I will be back out here to get you lickity-split. I don't think there are any more of them in there. I think they would have come out with the other two. But I will be super careful. We are going to stay together the whole time. You stay put and recover, ok? Promise? We'll be fine."

I pulled her face to mine and kissed her gently but deeply. When we parted I said, "I promise. Now hurry up."

She pulled out of the car and shut the door. I watched in the mirrors as they started up the stairs and she stopped at the top step. She turned around and walked to the rear hatch. I heard her open the back and I just watched her. She rummaged in one of the bags, shut the hatch and came back to my door. She opened it and handed me the clean handgun, a bottle of water and a bottle of Advil.

"Here you go. Just in case. And by the way, it *was* loaded," she said as she reached over and flipped off the safety. Then she handed me the water and Advil, "Take about six of these. We need to get the swelling down and get rid of that headache."

She again pulled out of the vehicle and shut the door behind her. I watched her climb the steps and approach the front door with the bat down by her side and something else in her other hand. When she got to the door, she leaned the bat up against the outside wall and performed a motion that immediately clued me in to what was in the other hand. She cocked the bloody gun she had taken with her.

I watched as she disappeared through the front door. Then Paul followed. Finally, Tammy walked through, but only after glancing back over her shoulder all around one more time. Then she was gone, too. I was all alone.

I began to slowly survey the viewable landscape. From where I sat, I could see for miles in three directions. There wasn't a tree in sight. Not to the right, left, or in front of me. Nothing was moving in any direction. The only place anything could be hiding was around the three vehicles in the driveway. There were two to the left and one to the right. The two on the left looked like they had been disused for years. The nearest one looked like an old Ford Pinto. Its hood was open and I could see there was nothing under it. That one at least was going to do us no good. The other two were both pickups. The one on the left was at least twenty years old, and I would have given even money that it wouldn't start. But the pickup on the right was a nice Ford F-250. A big Texas style truck if ever there was one.

I thought that I needed to make finding the keys to that truck a priority. I remembered that my iPhone has a notes app in it. It was sitting in the center console right where I had left it. I grabbed it, turned on the screen and hit the button for the notes app. I typed in my note. I added a couple other things that I wanted to make sure we did around here to make sure we were safe, and that is when I noticed the Wi-Fi symbol shining at me like a lighthouse beacon. I couldn't believe it. The cell towers were not responding, but the internet was still up, and as long as there was power here then I had a link to the web. My next thought was a truly joyful one. Ever the geek, I reasoned that if there is Wi-Fi, then there is a computer somewhere in there connected to the internet.

Jake! My mind screamed at me. I looked at the time display and it read 5:50. I quickly swiped through pages of apps until I found my favorite instant messenger application and tapped it. It popped open and displayed before me were all of my internet friends' screen names. All were grayed out; they were offline. The same as it had been for the past few days. *Come on, Jake! Come on, Jake! Come on, Jake!* I chanted in my head. Studio54Reject691 stayed grayed out. *Shit!*

I tossed the phone back in the center console and began to scan the area again. There really was nothing to see. Fields of plants low to the ground with long vines all around. I assumed they were watermelons in the summer, but now they were just a browning mess. The sun was shining brightly over the whole landscape. There were no cars down either stretch of road to the north or south. I could imagine how boring life in this place must be. There was nothing to do or see for miles.

Then my phone dinged. I looked at it in disbelief. It couldn't be a text message. I picked it up and stared at the instant messenger display.

Studio54Reject691: Steve, you there man?

I'm going to shorten the screen names now since I am hand writing this, but here is a full transcription of our conversation.

Me: Yeah man, I'm here.

Jake: Where's here? Did you not leave? I see your status. What the fuck's going on?

Me: We left. It's been rough. Could be worse though. We are on the road between SA and Houston. We are stopping for the night. A deserted farmhouse ala NotLD.

Jake: ??

Me: Jake, it was hell getting out of the city. Traffic on the highway was bad, and it wasn't moving. No one in the cars alive. Just like the movies. Fucking creepy.

Jake: ??

Me: Man of many words tonight I see. We are heading south to I-10 somewhere outside of SA. Hoping the vehicular carnage won't be as bad this far out. We've been taking farm roads east and don't want to travel at night.

Jake: Good idea.

Me: How are you guys holding up?

Jake: We're fine. The power went out again, this time for a couple hours before it came back on. I guess there aren't very many people left on the grid. But I don't think the grid is going to last much longer.

Me: Tell me about it. I am on my phone right now. No cell service, but the farmhouse has Wi-Fi. I haven't been inside to check for a computer yet, but there must be one. I think I may have a concussion. Fat zombie bitch fell on me.

Jake: LMFAO!!! You ok? Other than a little headache?

Me: Yeah. Wait til you see me.

Jake: My hero, gonna ride in on Xena and save the day huh?

Me: Jess is turning out to be the hero of the group. She and Tammy pulled the Zombie in the sundress off of me.

Jake: Tammy? What are you collecting a harem on your way?

Me: Haha, not quite. We picked up a couple as we were escaping the apartment complex. And boy am I glad to have them. Paul and Tammy.

Jake: Sweet. It'll be crowded here for all of you, but under the circumstances, the more the merrier.

Me: Agreed. You got your bug out bags ready?

Jake: Yeah, I already told you that.

Me: Oh, I must have been hit on the head or something. I forgot.

Jake: Ah. The bags are ready, but what are you planning? We're all going to hole up here right?

Me: I don't know man. I'm beginning to think that the best plan of action is to get the fuck out of Dodge. Big cities are bad. More people = more zombies. I like it out here. What do you think the odds are of convincing Janus to move to the country?

Jake: She's pretty freaked out as you can imagine. Very on edge. It won't be easy. Just get here and we can discuss it then.

Me: Ok man. That is the plan. I am going to rest here tonight. At first light we'll be on the road again, heading your way.

Jake: Can't wait to see you man. Stay safe.

Me: You too. Take care of yourself, sexy pants.

Jake: If anyone ever reads this they are totally going to think we are as gay as my neighbor here. You remember Big Gay Mark next door? LMAO!

Me: Yeah I remember. Take care. I gotta go, I am on guard duty.

Jake: Stay safe and get here!

That was definitely uplifting for me. My head ached, my legs hurt, but my spirit was as strong as ever. I looked at the display and saw it was ten past six. I decided to give them another five minutes and then I was going to honk the horn and go looking for them if they didn't come out. I opened the door after checking the side mirror just to make sure no zombies snuck up while I was typing.

It seemed I was still alone. It was getting hot as hell in the car. Stupid Texas extended summer. I opened the door and swung to a sitting position with my legs hanging out. That little effort threatened to make my head spin again so I stopped there. Besides, I had promised to stay in the car and keep watch. How could I just sit there? A quick look at the time and only a minute had passed. I leaned out of the car and tried to see inside the windows, but all I could see from my vantage point was half the house and all the windows had curtains. I spied no movement whatsoever.

I closed my eyes and listened. Straining to hear some sort of movement from within the house. All my ears would pick up over the ringing from my headache was the sound of grasshoppers all around. When I opened my eyes again I caught movement from my left at the front door of the house. A gloom was starting to settle in under the covered porch and I couldn't make out Jess until she was at the steps. I exhaled and saw that she was frowning at me.

"What the hell are you doing?" she asked in a very motherly tone.

"It's fucking hot in here with everything closed up. It was making my head hurt worse," I embellished to make my case. "I stayed in the car as promised. I just needed fresh air. I didn't want to pass out. Are you guys done in there?" I queried to get the subject off me.

"Yeah, we were just finishing up when we heard the car door open," she said. "You were going to come in and look for us weren't you?" Her tone slightly softened, but still had a hint of chastising in it.

"Not yet," I told her. "I was going to give you," I looked at the time, "another three minutes," and flashed her a guilty half smile. "There is nothing going on out here. What's it like in there. Did you find a computer?"

"Yes we did, and I knew you would want to use it, but when I turned it on there was a BIOS password protection on it. Can you get around that?" she asked.

"No, I'm not *that* tech savvy. I have plenty of friends who are. At least I used to. But their Wi-Fi is still working I can get on the net using my phone. I even chatted with Jake. They're doing fine. They're anxious for us to get there. I gave them a brief rundown of our situation and plan for tonight," I said with a bit of excitement in my voice.

Jess grinned and cocked her head a bit, "Should I be jealous of Jake? I mean you should tell me while our relationship is still new."

"Ha ha, very funny Jessica. He is my oldest friend and I love him very much. But you in that duct tape body armor are the sexiest thing I have ever laid eyes on," I told her sarcastically.

She was at the open car door now and stood before me with her hands on her hips and said, "Well mister, I am going to keep an eye on you two when we get there anyway, just to make sure." And she leaned in close and kissed me. Her tongue probed my mouth this time. Then she pulled away and whispered in my ear, "Call me Jessie, I love that."

"How about *my* Jessie," I whispered back in hers.

We were startled out of our "moment" by a loud clearing of the throat from the porch.

"Ok, you two, get a room. There are four to choose from upstairs. Two of them have beds big enough for two. Stephen, we want you to have the bigger bedroom. I don't think we can thank you enough for getting us out of San Antonio. We are forever in your debt. At least as long as we live," Paul said with an expression that started out kidding and moved to gratitude while he spoke.

"I'm no hero. We are all a team here. All I did was get us all together," I said matter-of-factly.

"You could have left us running through the mob of zombies. I think others would have," he said and actually shuddered.

Tammy was at his side nodding emphatically, "Please, Stephen, just accept our gratitude."

"Ok, but please, let's discuss it no more. We really are all equal here. I'm no leader," I said. "Can we unload what we need for tonight and leave the rest in here? My head and legs are killing me."

"Great idea," said Jess. *My* Jessie. "Paul, help me get him into bed upstairs, then we can unload."

Getting me up to bed took a while.

"Did any of you see a pad of paper and pen while you were looking around?" I asked. "I'd really like to write down the events of the day. It helps me sleep, and I'm afraid I am going to need all the help sleeping I can get."

"I saw one in the office downstairs," Tammy said and started for the stairs, stopped and turned to her husband. "Paul, would you come with me please?"

"Of course," he said dutifully.

They returned in a flash and here I sit writing while they bring in the bags with the guns and the groceries we plundered from the gas station. I heard them arm the car alarm and come back inside. I think I heard them locking the doors and turning out lights all around downstairs.

I really hope we don't have to board up the windows tonight. I think we'll be fine. I know one thing. I have a beautiful woman undressing in front of me right now, so it is time to put the pencil down. Good night, no one.

Wednesday, September 19, 2012 (handwritten)

What a day!

For starters, I didn't sleep well. Between the shooting pains in my head, the throbbing in my legs, and the nightmares, I think I only got two hours of good sleep. My only comforts were the packets of Advil on the bedside table, of which I popped two every time I woke up, and the warm body sleeping next to me. I'd like to say that I scored like the movie heroes no matter their injuries, but no. This isn't Hollywood, it's Central Texas, and I would have puked if I repeatedly jarred my head. So, for the fourth night in a row, I slept with this beautiful woman and did nothing more than sleep. At least the goodnight kiss was better than the previous nights, until the daggers jabbed my brain and I had to stop. I woke her up a couple times in the night fumbling for the drugs or snuggling back up with her.

I woke up spooning with Jess, *my* Jessie. My arm wrapped around her with my hand cupping her breast and the other arm under her pillow. That arm was quite numb. I didn't really want to move from that spot. Ever! But I had to urgently use the bathroom and my head was pounding rhythmically as if keeping time with a college marching band's drum line. I needed more drugs. *I can't drive to*

Houston today, I thought, rolling onto my back and wincing as the drums played on. Jess let out a moan as I lay flat. I lay there trying to wait out the pain, hoping it would subside if I were still. No luck. I pulled my arm out from under her and tried to lift it as the tingling started. It would not cooperate. I used my left hand to fumble for a couple more packets of Advil, but knocked them to the floor.

"Shit," I whispered.

"Baby, what'smatter?" She said as she rolled over and draped an arm across my chest. She didn't open her eyes. She only lay across me (and my dead arm) with all of her softness. Her head was on my shoulder and I turned and kissed the top of it.

"Baby, I need more drugs and I need to pee. It's light outside. We need to get started. I want to *try* to get to Houston and convince Jake's wife to come back here. Today if possible."

"Mmmmhmmm, but you feel so good," she said in a dreamy voice and her hand slid down from my chest under the covers. "See, you feel good. I want to." And she actually rolled on top of me. But as she dragged her leg over my ankle I winced and arched my back. "Oh baby, I'm so sorry," she said and slid off me, off the bed and to the floor. She knelt down and picked up the packets. She stood there next to the bed, opened them for me, handed the four pills to me and opened the water bottle. "What?" she asked.

"What, what?" I retorted. Snappy huh?

"You're staring," she said. The ghost of a grin beginning to form on her face.

"You, my love, are gorgeous. I can't wait to feel better. It felt so good to sleep with you last night," I said and winced as a fresh knife shot behind my eyes.

"Baby, you've slept with me for a few nights now," she said. The look on her face told me she knew exactly what I meant but wanted to hear me say it.

"Jessie, I don't know if it felt different to you, but knowing that you are mine makes all the difference. And by the way, I give myself to you. Can I have the water now?" I asked reaching my arm out toward her.

"I know," she held out the bottle for me to take. "And Stephen? I meant every word I said in the car yesterday. You really are everything I have wanted deep down. Thank you for coming for me. I will be your Jessie from now until the end of our days. And by the way, my body can't wait for you to be feeling better either. Now take those pills and let me play nurse," she grinned.

I dropped the four pills into my mouth and followed them down with a mouthful of water. The liquid made by bladder protest and I remembered that urgent need above the pain.

"I need to pee. More badly than I ever have in my life," I said and she could hear the urgency in my voice. She leaned down, kissed me quickly on the mouth and then pulled the blankets back.

"Oh my," she said her eyes lighting up as she beheld the effects of needing to urinate in the morning. After lingering on my groin for a moment her eyes tracked down to my legs and her expression turned from surprised delight to concern to mild horror. "Oh no, Stevey, your leg. You aren't going anywhere today. Probably not for a few days."

I slowly propped myself up on my elbows and immediately saw the source of the "Oh my" and the "Oh no." I'll leave the first to your imagination, but the second was my left ankle. I didn't know there were that many shades of black and blue. I slid that leg off the bed and to the floor. Then I followed it with the right leg. I worked myself into a sitting position.

"Oh dear God! I can feel the blood rushing down my leg," I hissed. I can't even describe how intense the pain was. It took a full minute for it to subside. It felt like a year.

Jess sat next to me, wrapped her arm around me and put my head against her chest. Under less painful circumstances, this would have been enjoyable, but with this amount of pain, I didn't even register where my head was. Tears streamed down my face. The pain in my head was all but forgotten.

When the pain subsided to a dull roar (I fully understand that phrase now), I sat back up. I took a deep breath and slid gingerly off the bed. I increased the weight on my feet by degrees, telling myself it was mind over matter. I need to do this. I need to drive about four hundred miles today. I need to get Jake and his family out of Houston. I stood fully and took another deep breath, moved my left foot forward a few inches and set it down. My right calf protested under my full weight but it was manageable. Then it was time to try the other leg. Not so good.

I swallowed a scream through gritted teeth and pursed lips and began to crumple under the pain. Jess was right there to catch me, slipping one arm around my torso, taking my weight. She helped me limp to the bathroom. My mind kept trying to control the situation. *I can still drive. I use my right leg to drive, not my left.*

I got to the toilet and relieved myself. Jess stood watching me with deep concern on her face. No dignity for the sick or injured. We've come a long way in one hundred or so hours.

"Jessie, can you check to see if the others are up? We need to have a 'family' meeting," I said. I hoped the guilt of what I was about to attempt didn't show on my face. Either it didn't, or she didn't catch it, because she turned with a nod. "Oh, and Jessie? Take the gun with you. From now on, always take the gun with you. Make sure it's loaded and with you. Please," I was sincerely pleading with her now.

"I will. And I'll be right back," she said. I watched her leave the bathroom and heard her getting dressed. *We are going to need more clothes and more duct tape. A lot of it.*

As soon as I saw her walk past the door, I braced myself with the bathroom sink and took one baby step after agonizing baby step. After about a dozen steps, I had gone the three feet to the sink. I leaned on my elbows and stared into the mirror. Two days of stubble covered my face. My eyes were puffy and sleep crusted. If I didn't know better, I would think I was one of *them*. My blue eyes still shone bright, in spite of current events. *This is not what a hero looks like.* The most prominent feature on my face was the huge bandage on my forehead. There was a small dot of red in the center of the two-inch white square taped to my skull.

I turned on the cold water and with my elbows still bracing me I scooped water into my hands under the faucet and lowered my face to them. It felt fabulously frigid. I rubbed at the corners of my eyes with my fingers. "I banish you crusties to the sewers or septic system below this house," and chuckled softly. There was pain, but it really was starting to subside. I lowered my head and dunked my face into the pool created by my hands once again. Sheer delight. There was a bottle of Listerine next to the sink and I grabbed it, twisted off the cap and took a mouthful straight from the bottle. I gargled and swished it around, feeling the burn, and spit it out into the basin. When I raised my head, Jess was standing beside me, dressed in duct tape from head to toe.

I grinned with guilt and said, "Hi."

"You really are bound and determined to be the hero here aren't you? Come on then manly man, let's get you dressed and downstairs. Paul and Tammy are up and ready for the family meeting. Plus there is something down there you need to see," she said with an odd mixture of reproach and admiration.

"I'm no hero. I will do whatever it takes to help those I love," I said as I lifted myself off my elbows to stand up straight. I turned toward her slowly, winced and grabbed her hand. "And

Jessie, that includes you. I may need you to drive today. I need to get to Jake. His wife is going to get him killed. I can feel it. I don't know how, but we need to get them out of there somehow. And soon. I need your help. Please," I begged.

"You stupid man. I know all of that. And of course I will be by your side for better or worse. I'll drive you there and back. If you need to drive to the moon, I'll go with you as well. And Stevie? I love you too," she said and pressed against me with her arms around my middle. She looked up at me and I kissed her.

For a moment of utter bliss there was nothing else in the world except the feel of her. Her lips against mine. Her arms wrapped around me. Her body pressed against mine. The duct tape was cold and not exactly comfortable, but it was real. It was a wonderful moment for me.

After we broke the embrace I let Jess help me to the bed, though I think I could have managed on my own. I let her dress me in my duct tape armor. I looked at her and down at myself. "What a pair we make. Like something out of a 1950's sci-fi movie. 'We come in peace Earthlings. We are here to eradicate your vermin zombie infestation,'" I said in my best (which isn't very good) robot voice. I chuckled, which turned into a laugh the more I thought it over. Jess laughed with me. It was a beautiful sound. I loved the combination of our laughter together. It really warmed my heart and motivated me for the day ahead.

"Shall we adjourn to the living room downstairs," I asked after we had stopped laughing long enough to speak. "Take me to your leader." That set us off on a fresh set of giggles. With her assistance and yet another quick kiss we went downstairs.

What they had to show me was truly interesting, and mildly troubling. But it gave me some fresh ideas to help us survive this thing.

It took a couple minutes to get down the stairs, but each step was easier than the one before. Jess was right by my side ready to catch me (or at least slow me down) if I fell. I insisted on using the banister and trying them on my own. All I could think on the way down was, *I ain't going back up there today.* I was just being dramatic, but it turned out I was right.

Paul and Tammy greeted us at the bottom of the stairs. They both had one finger up to their lips indicating that we should be quiet. I nodded and hobbled over to the window where they were motioning. They were peeking through wood-slat blinds in the living room. When I got there, I slid two slats apart and put my face to them.

I looked out toward the front yard and saw Xena's back end (not nearly as nice as Jess', but I digress) and a scene of carnage near the driver's side. At first, I didn't take everything in. I could see three more zombies out there and they appeared to be eating what was left of the male farmer zombie (for lack of a name). The female farmer zombie was completely untouched and lay still just a couple yards away. There were also several other shapes around that had been torn apart and eaten as well. I couldn't make out what those were, but based on the fur and feathers scattered around, they had been animals of some kind. I watched in horror as they tore flesh from the farmer's legs. One of the zombies sat in the bloody dirt cross-legged with the farmer's leg in her hands, which still had its work boot and sock on. This zombie appeared to be having a picnic in the yard. But instead of fried chicken, she was eating the raw meat of a former zombie. There wasn't much left of the man. His caved in skull appeared to be in pieces and no brain matter inside. There were bones picked clean all around.

My eyes kept returning to the big zombie that squashed me like a bug. There didn't seem to be any damage to her. Her neck bent back at an unnatural angle but that was all I could see. These new zombies hadn't touched her at all. Why? Then I noticed why. Her mouth was still moving. It was a bloody gaping hole – presumably from the bat – but her jaws were opening and shutting. This was most interesting to me.

My eyes left these poor wretches and scanned the horizon that was visible from this window. There were figures shambling toward the house outlined by the sun from behind. One was at the end of the driveway. Three were walking along the road from the north.

I felt a tap on the shoulder and Paul motioned to the couch. The four of us sat and began to discuss in hushed tones. Paul started.

"I've been watching them since dawn," he said. "Did you see the animal carcasses?"

I nodded.

"Coyote. They didn't kill it. They ate it, same with the crows and one vulture. The animals were already dead when the first of the zombies showed up at our doorstep. They never once tried to get in here. They went straight for the easy meal. We didn't finish off the big one and they are leaving her alone. I find that odd. What do you think?" he put the question out there for anyone, but he was looking right at me.

"I don't know. They won't kill their own kind, but they will eat them if they are already dead. We saw it yesterday at the gas station, too. God was that only yesterday? Anyway, they seem to prefer living human flesh but in the absence of that, they'll eat any dead – truly dead – flesh. They'll eat the flesh of animals as well. They don't limit themselves to human or once-human meat. They didn't kill the animals, so we don't know if they fall into the category with humans – whom they will catch, kill and eat – or other zombies – that they will only eat if already dead. If I had to guess, I would say lump the animals in with the humans. Not that it really matters right now. How did the animals die though? Could the zombie meat be poisonous to them? If so, why weren't there more coyotes dead? Don't they usually hunt in packs?" I paused for a moment and Tammy jumped in on the conversation.

"It looked extremely skinny. It's possible it was a lone dog. It's possible the rest of its pack sensed the danger in the flesh. Darwin weeding out the weak," she said.

I said, "Could be either, or both. Both those ideas are better than anything I can come up with – which is nothing. Do we go on the assumption that the flesh is poisonous until proven otherwise?" I asked and looked at each of them. They all nodded. "Ok, how can we use this to our advantage? Off the top of my head, we can use the dead undead to keep the living undead (I shook my head slightly at the words I had actually said) away from the house. Put them out on the road and down a ways. Close enough to see them coming in, yet far enough to live here undetected. And that is assuming they don't have super senses. We know they don't have above average hearing or they would have been knocking to get in here. Same thing with smell. They do seem to use sound as a way to locate humans. Especially car sounds. If a car is running, they come a-shambling. Could that be a vibration thing? I guess it doesn't really matter. Cars draw them to us. Where was I? Oh yeah, we don't know about their vision yet. But I'm sure it won't take long to figure that out. Am I missing anything?" I asked.

Jess spoke up and both Paul and Tammy were visibly grateful when she did. I could tell I may not like what she was going to say. "We think that Paul and Tammy should stay here and keep the house safe for when we get back tonight or tomorrow," she said and hurried to continue before I could interject. "We don't want to get back and have the place overrun with those things and then have to find a new place to stay. This place seems perfect, and I think we should keep it that way. Like you said, we can see them coming from a long way off, and they seem to be trickling in a couple at a time, not in huge numbers like in the city." When she said that her face went grey, and I'm pretty sure it was because of where we proposed to go today. Hell, I might as well tell it like it is – where *I* was going to lead us today. I was asking her to drive right into the mouth of danger. I felt my face grow hot with shame for needing to do this. She grabbed my hand and squeezed it. "We have to. I understand that. It scares me, but I understand that," she said and completely disarmed my shame. "They can set up these ones as bait to keep the rest away from the house, maybe set up a ring of them or something, I don't know. Pick them off one by one and keep them away. We'll be back with the other four tonight, we'll have more help and can come up with a grand plan for continued survival. I know there is strength in numbers, but there would be eight of us if Paul and Tammy went. Your car only holds five safely. If they don't go then only one person has to ride the two hundred miles back here in the back of your car. That won't be a very comfortable ride for one. Three riding in that uncomfortable, small space, would be horrible. And we…" I cut her off then.

"I see the value in this plan. I really do. I also would like to point out that I am not a dictator here. You voluntarily came with me – all three of you. I voluntarily brought you along with me. I am not going to hold you to any sort of obligation or commitment. You seem to be looking to me as the leader. So be it. As leader, I give you each – even you," I looked at Jess, "the right and option to not go along with anything I say if you don't see the value in it. I know I'm not perfect. I value equally the knowledge each of you possess. You each have emotions and survival instincts. I am not going to assume mine are better than yours. I know my instincts are screaming at me to stay here and not go anywhere near another big city. Unfortunately, I can't listen this time. I don't blame you for listening to your instincts. I hope to be here for each of you when you need me most, and when the time comes, that you will return the favor. That said, here," I spread my arms and motioned to the house "is where we would all like to be, right?"

They all nodded in agreement.

"Then I will not demand, nor even ask any of you to leave now. Let's come up with a plan to get those three off our front lawn; front dirt, rather," I paused for one breath and Tammy came across from the opposite couch toward me. I could see tears in her eyes starting to spill over.

"Thank you, thank you, thank you! I promise we'll keep it safe for you to come back to," she whispered and hugged me and kissed my cheeks. In the process, she also bumped my swollen ankle, and I winced.

"Shhhhhhh, Tammy, Tammy, Tammy! There's no need. Stop. You're hurting me," I said, trying to keep my voice down but still be heard over her. She heard the last part and saw me wince. She shot back off me as if pulled by a bungee, sat back down next to Paul, grabbed his hand and squeezed. There was a non-stop stream of tears pouring from her eyes.

I started again, "We need to take care of the three – probably four now in the front yard. We need to get you two armed with more than just baseball bats. As we saw yesterday, that can be a problem. But I think they are still the best bet. They are a hell of a lot quieter than a firearm. If I were you, I would save the guns for emergencies only. I'm going to leave all but a couple days' worth of food here for you two. It should last you at least a week. And if we're not back by then, you will need to come up with your own plan. Is that fair?" I asked.

"More than fair," Paul said. "Just make sure you're safe and if you can make it back here, then do it. We are already better off than we were in the apartment."

"Fair enough. I've made my decision. I want to be here and if I can convince my buddy's wife to come, then I will. I am not staying in Houston like she wants. Too much can go wrong in the big city. I know how you two feel. I don't *want* to go to Houston, but Jake has been my best friend since I was eight years old. His kids are my godkids, and I was the best man at their wedding. Hell, I even dated his wife before she dumped me for him.

"Now, that pickup out there. Did any of you find keys that may go to it?" I asked.

"There were a bunch of keys on a board in the kitchen," Paul said. "They weren't labeled, but I'm sure one of them works for it."

"Great! My feeling on using the truck is about the same as using the guns. I suggest last resort only. I know when we get back I am not going to be starting a car again for quite some time. They are too loud in this new ultra quiet world. That leads me to my next request. If you two have to bug out, please try to leave a note telling us where you are trying to get to so we can try to follow when we get back. But don't leave the note where anyone can find it easily. Put it under your pillow. If we get back and that pickup is gone, the first place I will go is to your bed to find that note telling me why you left and where you went. Could you do that for me if you have to leave and it is safe to do so? If the note will mean the difference between life and death, then flee toward life. If that happens, I'm sure there will be enough clues around to let me know why you left. Am I missing something?" I asked.

Tammy asked timidly, "Won't they hear you leave and come from miles around to investigate?"

"Potentially yes, but I am going to take care of the ones we can see now to the north. I counted only a few. And any between here and I-10 I will take care of. If I miss any of those, they should follow us away from here at least. So, with any luck you won't have to worry about any of them from the south until we come back. We will try to take care of any of them we see on the way back in. I'm not saying it's foolproof, it's the best I've got though."

"I don't have a better idea. Thank you for doing what you can for us. Paul's right, it is better here than where we were."

"Okay, first things first," I said. "How do we get rid of the ones in the front? I won't be much help with these legs."

"We could weight down the corners of a sheet and drop it over them from on top of the porch. You can get onto it from our room," Paul said.

"Not bad, but do we know how strong this porch is? I really don't want someone to fall off or through it. One gimp is bad enough," I said apologetically.

Jess said, "Why not just open the door and invite them on in? They don't move that fast and they can't come up the steps more than single file because your car is in the way. If we're lucky, they will trip trying to get up the stairs and we brain them. If not, we still only have to deal with them one at a time. Stephen, you can try to distract as many as you can away from the steps where they can't reach you. That way we won't have a repeat of yesterday with more than one coming at once. And at least this time we have the high ground."

"General Jessie to the rescue," I said and grinned at her. "It's brilliant. Then we toss them all in the pickup, find the keys and drive them down the road, taking out those other three in the process. Stick together on this one. Get us on the road and back home safely tonight or tomorrow." In the back of my head as I finished this monologue I heard Jake add, *Don't forget to kill Phillip.* I let out a snort and grabbed a pillow to cover my face. It hurt like hell when it hit my forehead, but I couldn't restrain the laughter. When it subsided, I pulled the pillow down and, as expected, everyone was staring at me. "Sorry, just had a funny thought about a zombie movie. My rundown of the plan just reminded me of it. That's all. Are we ready? Give me a head start, it's going to take me a bit to get to the door."

Jess helped me up and that painful sensation of blood rushing down my veins hit me again. I doubled over with my hands on my knees. Then the blood ran to my head, causing the knives to pierce my skull again.

"Fuck me," I hissed.

Jess was right there at my side steadying me. She whispered in my ear away from the others, "I tried, remember?" She kissed my ear and helped me stand up again when the pain subsided.

I started out with baby steps again, but the recovery was much quicker than first thing out of bed. By the time I got to the door, I was more or less walking like one of the undead outside – short shambling steps.

We looked out the blinds and saw the same scene as before with a couple differences. There was very little flesh left on the bones of the farmer zombie. The undead zombies were picking through the bones and blood trying to find bits of flesh. There were also now four of them instead of three picking through the bones. The female zombie was wandering around aimlessly, bending down to pick up a crow carcass or to grab at a leg bone sticking out of a work boot.

"Bats ready?" I whispered to everyone.

I waited until I heard an affirmative from everyone, took a deep breath and pulled the door wide open. The sunlight streamed into the house. It dazzled my eyes, but I stepped out onto the porch. I looked left and right and saw no movement as my eyes adjusted to the glare. I moved left along the porch, watching as the four zombies noticed me and immediately started walking toward me. I passed the steps down to the yard and walked along the porch so that when the four zombies came at me, they weren't able to get me. All four of them walked to the front of the porch instead of the steps. Out of the corner of my eye I saw the others come onto the porch with me. I waited a second for their eyes to adjust to the morning sunshine in their faces.

I had four zombies reaching through the wooden verticals of the porch at me. But none of them had any reasoning skills, so they were not trying to figure out how to get at me. They were just trying to take the straightest line to the meal. I took the opportunity to do a little damage while I had their attention. I lifted the bat above my head and brought it down on one arm. The swing was weak and it made my head ache when it connected with the creature's forearm. The jarring shot up my arms, through my shoulders and into my head. The up side was that the zombie's forearm was now hanging down at a ninety-degree angle to the rest of the outstretched arm. I moved to the side of the arms and lined up to take a swing at as many arms at once as I could. Again, I raised the bat and brought it down. This time I connected with three arms. Two broke and fell completely limp. One of the forearm bones broke through the skin. No blood came out of the wound when the white bone pierced the skin. The third zombie in the group was the tallest and his head was level with the banister running the length of the porch. I didn't know if I would do enough damage to kill it, but if I could put it down for a moment when Jess and the others started luring them up on the porch, it would be one less to worry about all at once.

I turned and faced it. It continued to reach for me through the porch but got no closer to me. I raised the bat and brought it down harder than the two previous swings. I connected with the fat of the bat dead center in the top of its skull. I saw it collapse inward and the zombie went down in a heap. My own head protested from the effort and I stumbled back against the house, bat clanging to the porch beside me. Each stumble shot lightning bolts up my legs and I cried out in agony.

"Stay there," Jess shouted at me.

I could only watch as the other three all turned to face her. Once they saw her, they began to shuffle toward the steps. What happened next was almost scripted. Almost comical. Almost Shaun of the Dead. They came at the steps single file. Jess was right behind Xena at the top of the steps. She was directly in their line of sight. Paul and Tammy were side by side facing down the steps.

I saw this set up as a recipe for disaster. Someone on our side was going to get hit in the back of the head with a bat.

"Listen guys! Paul you swing first. Jess wait until he is back then you swing. Tammy, you wait until Jess is back then you swing. Got it guys? Paul, Jess, Tammy! Paul, Jess, Tammy," I barked at them. I wanted to give it the authority of an order. I was hoping they would respond as if it were such.

It was perfect. The first zombie got to the steps and after the first attempt to walk straight at Jess and its feet meeting the front of the bottom step, it looked down and adjusted the height it raised its foot. Paul swung before it even raised its head again. Its head exploded. Brains sprayed the side of my car and the porch. Paul pulled the bat away, bits of skull, brain and hair dropped from the barrel. The zombie fell forward onto the steps. That's when this would have been comedic if it had been a movie and not real life.

"Reset! Paul, get ready, you're up again!" I barked at him. "All of you get ready. There's two more! And they're coming to eat you. Get ready!"

They all raised their bats in unison. The next zombie at the steps was the leg-eating female. She was not quite as coordinated as the first one. Her leading foot hit the front of the bottom step and she tumbled forward toward Jess. Jess was well out of the way, but this sudden change in head location caused Paul's swing to hit the zombie in the back. She only had one good arm thanks to my second whack at them and she tried to use it to crawl the rest of the way up the step.

As soon as Paul pulled his bat back, I yelled, "Jess, now!" She swung her bat down with all her might, connecting with the zombie's skull with a sickening crunch. But it didn't cave in completely and she kept advancing toward Jess. "Jess, back!" She did as I instructed and even as I was about to yell for Tammy, she was already arcing her bat down on the back of the zombie's head. This time it caved in completely. "Back Tammy! Reset! One more, get ready! Paul you first!"

The fourth zombie was walking with his arms outstretched, even though both were broken halfway down each forearm. This one tripped over the legs of the female that had just perished. It tumbled forward, but this one's trajectory didn't send it up the stairs, it went face first into the side of Xena. Its arms flailed about, forearms flopping uncontrollably. After it hit the car, it slid down and had trouble getting up without the use of its arms. Paul didn't wait for it to figure it out. He jumped the three steps down to the dirt, spun to face the house parallel with the car, raised his bat and swung it down with a battle cry. He connected the first time with the back of its skull, which instantly became mush. He spun around looking throughout the yard, but the closest one of them was still a quarter mile down the road.

With the immediate danger over, Tammy dropped her bat, stepped over the fallen undead on the steps and hugged Paul tight. His arms were at his side, the bat in a death grip in his right hand, barrel on the ground. He was still trying to look all around them while Tammy sobbed into his chest. I leaned back against the window and slid down until my rear was sitting on the window sill. I dropped my throbbing head into my hands and listened to my own heartbeat in my ears.

I could hear Jess's footsteps coming toward me slowly. She was breathing heavily. The adrenaline was still coursing through her. When she stopped in front of me, I raised my head and looked up at her.

I couldn't manage to raise my voice again, so what I said then came out in a hoarse voice that I didn't recognize, "Fuck Xena, you are my warrior princess." I almost saw it too late. Another zombie had come up the steps on the other side of the car and was reaching for Jess. I leapt up and loped beside her, pushing the thing in the chest with both my hands, my legs screaming for mercy, but that little momentum carried the zombie and me back toward the recent battle zone. One of its legs caught on one of its fallen comrades and its upper half fell backward. I went down on top of it. I bounced to the side toward the house and couldn't believe what I saw. It was lying across another zombie and brains dripped out the back of its head. It had fallen on the tow hitch of my car. Its weight and mine drove the steel ball into the back of its skull.

I lay there in agony, "Jessie," I croaked. I pointed to the other side of the car. "More?"

Jess jumped over the pile of bodies, went to the other side of the Xterra and peered around it from the top of the porch. "No more baby. Just the ones down the road." She lifted my arms, put them around her neck and lifted me to a sitting position.

I was breathing as heavy as the rest of them at that point. That last bit was all the strength I had left.

"Stephen, you may not think of yourself as a hero, but you are really my hero. That's another time that I would have died if you hadn't saved my ass," she said

"Jessie," I started, but she stopped me with a kiss. A deep kiss. When she stopped I said, "I was just going to ask for more drugs. And maybe some Tequila. I hurt a little bit."

"I can help with the drugs, but haven't seen any booze in a while. A margarita sounds heavenly right now. I'll be right back," she said and kissed me on the cheek. To the others she said, "Can you guys keep an eye on him a minute, please?" With that, she turned and strode into the house.

Paul and Tammy started walking around the dead zombies and up the stairs toward me. They were taking great care not to slip in the mess.

"Listen you guys," I started. "I'm sorry for acting like a drill sergeant. I could just envision so many things going wrong if we weren't careful. I really am sorry to have acted like that."

Paul looked at me a moment as if trying to choose his words exactly right. "You acted in what you thought was our best interest. We understand that. It's ok man. Nice save there at the end. I'm impressed." I would have sworn I heard a tone of condescension in his voice. I smiled as if I didn't catch it.

"Help me up?" I asked extending my arms to them. They each took one and pulled me to my feet. I immediately doubled over in agony from my legs and my head. With my hands on my knees, I surveyed the carnage on the porch and in the yard. "Let's load up the corpses into the pickup first, then split the supplies. After that, we drive these bodies, what, half a mile down the road and dump them as bait for any others that come by and take care of those ones?" I pointed at the four that were now walking in from the north. Then we will head south, and get back here as soon as humanly possible."

"Sounds like a plan to me," Paul said.

I bent down and grabbed the zombie by the hair that had impaled his head on my tow hitch and yanked. There was a squelching sound and I let its head fall to the porch. I leaned on the back of my car with my head on my forearms. I closed my eyes and breathed through the pain in my legs and head, trying to believe there was no slight in Paul's tone and words. Has he already decided that this house was his instead of all of ours? Is he going to give us problems when we get back? Surely, I'm imagining things. The four of us have made an effective team thus far. I am really looking forward to getting back here with four more people, two of whom will make a great addition to this team.

Are these two going to be able to hold this house for even a day or two? I guess there is only one way to find out. I am going to give them every advantage I can think of to do it, but not to my detriment.

When Jess came out I gave her a big hug and whispered in her ear, "Please go along with whatever I am about to do. Trust me."

She squeezed me back and replied, "Yes, is something wrong?"

"Beginning of something maybe. Not going to take any chances. Our survival is number one to me. So I am going to do something that I wouldn't normally do. I am hoping no one notices. Please be careful."

"Of course baby, just tell me what you need me to do," she said and kissed me on the cheek.

"Can't, love. Don't know how or when I'm going to do it. I will just have to seize the opportunity when it comes. You roll with me and trust in me, please."

She took my cheeks in her hands and stared directly into my eyes and said, "Stephen, I don't know how to tell you this, but I am with *you* from now on. Partners for as long as we live. Need I go on?"

"No, I am just feeling like, if I'm wrong, then I am being a dick, but if I am right and don't act, then I screwed you and me. And that is even less cool. So, there, I've warned you, I may do something that is contrary to what I may be saying or to what you might expect of me."

"Baby, you do what you need to and I will help you any way I can. I'll help us any way I can." She kissed me and together we walked off the porch toward where Paul and Tammy were starting to move the dead Zombies toward the back of the pickup. She handed me four Tylenol, two Advil and a small bottle of water. I downed them and attempted to help the others get the bodies into the pickup.

I helped as best I could. It was pure agony on my legs to help lift those corpses into the back of the pickup but I didn't complain. I just kept helping. When all but the fat one were in the back, I walked back to where she lay, still gnashing her jaws. I stood there looking at her, and she looked at me with the one eye that was skyward. "Is this really what your life has become?" I asked her. Then I brought the bat down sharply on her head, ending her undeath. "How the hell are we going to get you out of here?"

Bungee cords turned out to be the answer. It wasn't pretty, but then again we were talking about zombies in the first place, so pretty was out the window right off the bat. We couldn't lift her into the bed of the truck, so we hooked bungee cords that I had in the back of Xena around her middle and to the tow hitch of the pickup. She left quite a trail of gore from the driveway to where we cut her loose. But I am getting ahead of myself here.

After we loaded up the corpses, I told Paul and Tammy that I had the bungees in the car and I would be right back. Amazingly, it didn't take much subterfuge to go into my car unattended. I had to go into the house to get the keys, and stopped and grabbed the bag full of weapons we brought into the house last night. I carried it outside and set it down behind the car. I opened the back and tossed it in beside the bags of other supplies from my apartment. I grabbed the bungees and returned to the others.

On my way back to them, I had a change of heart that I still can't explain. "Hey guys would you come over here a minute and help me?"

"Sure," they all said in one form or another and started walking toward the porch.

"Before we get that mess off of our lawn, let's get the supplies sorted out. That way we can get on the road as soon as that end of the road is clear," I said as we reached the back of my car. "Can we have a bag of waters for the road, there and back?" I asked as I pulled the bag of guns out and lay it on the ground again. I unzipped it, pulled out one of the rifles and handed it to Paul.

"Tammy go get him a bag of waters, please," Paul asked his wife. After she was gone, he said to me, "Thank you for this." He held up the gun. "I know you don't have to do this."

"I'm not done, Paul. Consider it good faith. I want you to be able to defend this place. I want you to live. I really consider us a team. And you are responsible for holding down this fort for us all." I reached into the bag and pulled out all the rifle shells, split them into two piles very deliberately and pushed half to his feet. I looked up at him from where I was kneeling. "Jessie, would you mind if we left them your gun? We'll still have another one just like it."

"Of course honey," she said without hesitation. She reached behind her, brought it out and handed it over to Paul. She must have had it in her waistband back there. This woman amazes me more every day I know her. More like every hour I know her.

I then split the handgun ammunition and put ours back in the bag with the shotgun and the other rifle. True to my word, I kept only enough food for the two of us for a couple days and left the rest here. I also pointed out the printouts I had made a couple days before and suggested that he look at them. "There is some pretty interesting reading in there. A lot of it we are going to need in the coming months, I think."

With the water in the back seat with the guns and food, we were ready to get this show on the road again. It was now mid-morning and I didn't want to wait much longer to start out for Houston.

We found the keys to the pickup, secured the bungees to the back and around the big zombie, and the two vehicles started off north up the road, Tammy and I driving each truck. The first of the zombies was almost to the driveway, and as discussed, Tammy drove a short distance past it and we stopped just short of it. Paul and Jess jumped out and approached it from opposite sides. The first one started toward Jess, so Paul swung his bat at it from behind, dropping it to the pavement. Jess finished the job with one more swing to the back of its head.

They loaded it into the truck with the others, got in and we continued down the road. The next one was a woman and we employed the same strategy against her. This time, after Jess and Paul got out the zombie turned toward Paul as they approached from opposite sides. Jess took the first swing and Paul the second. This strategy worked like a charm each time. By the time the house was about three quarters of a mile behind us we came to the last of the zombies. This time they killed it and left it on the side of the road where it fell. Tammy and I got out and helped unload of the pickup.

When we finished the job, there was a pile of truly dead zombies on the side of the road. We unhooked the big one and rolled her to the pile as well.

I looked at Paul and he looked a bit afraid when he saw that I was really about to depart. "Paul, take care of yourselves. Keep the house if you can. But if it comes down to the house or your lives, get the hell out of here. Keep some supplies in the cab of the truck in case you need to get out quick. I guess that's all I can say, besides be as quiet and inconspicuous as possible and be careful. We'll be back soon. I don't know if we'll make it back today, but hopefully by tomorrow. If something happens to us, thank you for your help and trust."

Tammy grabbed me at this point and wrapped me in a bear hug that was actually very comforting. I put my arms around her as well and hugged her as if I were never going to see her again. Who knows, I may not. Then Paul came over and put his arms around Tammy and me. Jess came up and completed the group hug by wrapping her arms around Tammy and Paul. After a few moments, we broke the embrace and Paul broke the silence, "Until tonight then?"

I grinned at that and he returned the grin. And that was all that needed to be said. If he had slighted me earlier, it was in the past and a non-issue. We got back in the car around 10:30 in the morning. I asked if Jess would mind driving, and she said of course not. We put the bats on the floor behind our seats where we could get to them easily and down the road we went. When we got back in front of the farmhouse, we slowed and both raised our arms out the windows and waved. We saw the gesture returned as Tammy and Paul pulled into the driveway. We continued driving south toward I-10.

***

We only passed two farmhouses between the main highway and our house. This was exactly what we hoped to see. We only had to stop three times to dispatch zombies in the road, employing a similar strategy to the one we used before. Jessie would stop ten to fifteen feet in front of them. We would get out, grab the bats and wait on both sides of the truck. Whichever side of the car they went to, the other of us would come up behind them and bash them from behind. This strategy worked beautifully against one at a time. I'm not sure how we were going to handle many at once.

That would come soon enough. We were not traveling particularly fast. Jess was bopping along at only thirty-five on the country road. This was alright with me. I was eager to get to Jake, but I was also very afraid to drive back into a big city. San Antonio may seem tame by comparison. We just didn't know at the time what we would be driving into.

The drive started out uneventful enough. Once we got to I-10, we had an issue getting on the freeway, but once we abandoned the conventional lanes of traffic and just went wherever we needed to, we had little trouble navigating; a curb here, a median there. Eastbound in the westbound lanes on occasion was common. We saw several zombies, but didn't bother to stop to dispatch them. They were not an issue for us, so we just kept on trucking eastward. We stopped roughly an hour after getting onto I-10 in order to relieve ourselves along the side of the highway with not a car or zombie in sight. The congestion of dead cars lessened to nothing the farther east we went. However, there were increases of zombies and dead cars with each small town we passed.

Somewhere around a small town called Flatonia about halfway to Houston, Jess asked me, "Do you think they are going to make it until we get back?"

"I really have no idea. I certainly hope so. I want them to be there when we get back. That's why I changed my mind about the guns at the last minute. I thought they had a 50-50 chance of making it, and I didn't want to lose those two guns. But then again, I wanted to increase their chances of survival. In the end I went with what my conscience, and not the survivalist in me, told me was right. I'm going on gut instinct here," I said.

"Your instinct has worked so far. How are your legs and head?" she asked.

"Pretty good at the moment. I dread getting out and walking again. That hurt like hell when we got out to piss. How are we on gas?" I asked, changing the subject.

"We've got a little more than half a tank. How far can we get on that?" she asked me.

"We're going to have to find a way to siphon one of these cars into this one. Unfortunately, a hose is not something I keep in my car to handle such things. I have a one gallon gas can back there, but we need a hose either way if we are siphoning. Take the next access road, baby, please. I want to find a house that is isolated and easy to scope out from a distance. I just want to get in, grab a hose and get out."

"You got it honey," she said and took the next exit.

A tailor-made farmhouse was immediately following the exit. The house was only twenty yards off the road and we could see most of the area around the front yard. It appeared to be zombie free.

"Drive all the way up to the front of the house. I'm looking for a garden hose."

She did as I asked without a word. We were both trying to look everywhere at once. She pulled up to the front of the house and I saw the faucet to the right of the porch. I got out, grabbed my bat and walked over to the faucet while Jess stood with her back to me keeping an eye on the house. The hose had apparently not been removed in years. It was completely crusted with lime and wouldn't turn.

"Shit! I need a knife out of the car," I said. I stood up to go, but Jess motioned for me to stop.

"I'll get it. Where is it?" she asked me.

"It's in the center compartment between the driver's and passenger's seat. There is a Leatherman there that would be perfect," I said.

"Got it," she said as she turned and took the two steps before opening the driver's door. I turned back to the hose to try to twist it off one more time. Behind me, I heard her rummage in the center console and then, "Found it."

I heard the door close and I stood up and turned to the car. There were two of *them* just a few feet away from Jess. I rushed forward, the adrenaline overcoming the pain yet again. I took a loping swing at the head of the zombie on my right and connected causing it to stumble to the left and into the other zombie just as Jess dropped the Leatherman and raised her bat over her head. Both of the zombies crashed into the hood of the car.

The one I hit fell to the ground and began to get up. The other one looked down at the first, as if assessing whether this obstacle was food or not. It quickly decided that the downed zombie was not food and recommenced walking toward Jess. I sighed and cocked my bat back for another swing. That was when I saw the bat come arcing down from the other side of the zombie, smashing dead center in the head. This zombie crumpled to the ground as well. I adjusted my target and swung at the head of the zombie trying to get up. Like a baseball on a tee, I smashed the bat squarely into the back of its head. It flew into the ground face first and didn't move.

"I feel like I'm fucking Barry Bonds minus the steroids. If you come across any of those in the next couple of days, I think I am going to want them to bulk up if we are going to be taking care of these things like this. I like that it's fairly quiet, but my muscles are starting to protest," I said breathing heavily.

"Yeah, and we aren't using our ammo. That is a very good thing as well. I have a feeling there will come a point when we are going to need every round we can spare. So while we are faced with onesie, twosies, we should keep using the bats," she said as I walked up to her.

I planted a kiss on her mouth to silence her. When we parted, I said, "I know honey, I was just being a whiney bitch. That's all."

"Kinda, yeah," but she had a big grin on her face as she said it. She bent and retrieved the Leatherman from the dirt and handed it to me. "Now, where the hell did they come from?" she asked looking behind me.

Her eyes went wide and I spun to see another one of them. This one was sitting on the top step of the porch. She had on a black t-shirt, black jeans, black shoes and socks, long jet-black hair, pale face and dark sunken eyes. She held a cigarette in her right hand, and while we looked at her, she put it to her lips and took a deep drag off it. She regarded us with curiosity. She couldn't have been more than sixteen or seventeen when she died. The cigarette perplexed me. The fact that she wasn't coming at us added to my confusion.

I walked toward her and pulled the bat back for a swing. When I got to her, she calmly raised her left hand and pointed a handgun at my face. That stopped me before the swing got going and the head of the bat fell to the ground. I'm sure I looked like a fucking idiot at that point. I certainly felt like one. I was completely puzzled.

"You're not one of them?" I asked, motioning to the zombies on the ground near my car.

She just stared at me, with a mixture of curiosity and growing amusement. A grin spread across her face. "I do look like one of them don't I? I think maybe it's time for a new look. To answer your question, yes and no. I'm not a walker, but those were my parents you just killed for good."

"Shit," I said. "I'm so sorry, they were coming at us. We had to…" I stopped mid-sentence, because she was actually laughing at me. "Did I miss a joke?"

"Well, no. You are apologizing for something I should have done days ago, tried to do yesterday, and discovered I didn't have the balls to do. I'm not upset at you. My friends would definitely be calling me a pussy right now. I was always talking big about hating my parents, and when I finally get a legitimate excuse to take them out, I couldn't do it. Some tough Goth chick, huh? I guess I'm all talk. I should thank you for doing that for me."

"Please, don't thank us for that. I feel horrible about doing it. Every time I do it, actually. Even though I know it's them or me, it doesn't make it any easier. I have to disassociate myself from the act. I have to make it feel like a video game. I'm Stephen. This is Jessica. What's your name?" I asked extending my hand to her. Jess was standing beside me with a grin on her face.

"I'm Abigail, but everyone calls me Casper," she said shaking my hand. It was quite a delicate hand, both small in size and frail in firmness. She looked me in the eyes and gave me a huge smile. Then she looked at Jess, extended her hand to her and said, "What's so funny?"

"He was going to hit you with the bat. He actually thought you were one of them. I know our nerves are on edge, but you are obviously not a zombie," she said and shook her hand briefly. "Come here." She pulled Abigail into her and gave her a big hug.

I stood there with my mouth open and gawked at what I was witnessing. At first, Abigail went rigid with her arms at her side. Clearly, she wasn't used to this sort of affection, but slowly, as if she were an ice cube melting in a glass of whisky, she began to soften. Her arms slowly raised to Jess' side, then wrapped around her completely. She buried her head against Jess' chest, her hair falling around her face. Before long, I could see her body hitching, and hear her sniffling. Embarrassed to be witnessing this, I looked around in a half serious attempt to see if there were any more of *them* around. When I didn't see any, I left the porch and the two women embracing. Before I did, I saw that there were tears falling from Jess' eyes as well. Abigail was sobbing and Jess was crying. They seemed to be comforting each other.

I turned and went back to the hose. I opened the knife attachment and began to cut through the hose just past the base. I contemplated how long I wanted between cuts. When I couldn't decide on a length, I decided that thirty feet of hose may come in handy. I wound up putting the entire length of hose in the back of Xena.

After I closed the back of the car, I walked back to the porch. The women were composing themselves. Apparently, this was one of those female bonding experiences. I walked up to them and asked, "Abigail, would you like to come with us? We found a place outside of San Antonio. We are going to Houston to get a friend of mine and his family and then heading back there. You are more than welcome to join us. The more the merrier, or safety in numbers if you like that saying better."

She jumped off the porch, threw her arms around my neck and hugged me hard, pulling me down to her height, which was only about five feet. "Thank you, Stephen. Thank you, thank you, thank you." And she started to cry again. "I loved my parents. I was so mean to them. I treated them like shit and now they're dead. Let's get out of here. Please."

"Ok, have you got anything that you want to take?" I asked. "A couple changes of clothes? We don't have much in the way of toiletries, but this seems like a good place and time to stock up if you have them. How close is your nearest neighbor?"

"Over a mile down the access road. And you've come to the right place for supplies. My parents were Sam's Club freaks, and they went just last weekend. So we have everything we needed for the next two months. Let me show you," she said. She kissed me on the cheek before releasing me from the hug, then turned and ran up the porch and into the house.

I looked at Jess and mouthed, *bipolar?* She just shrugged back and we followed Abigail into the house. It looks like we are going to be surrogate parents to a teenager during the zombie apocalypse. Something that I think would be difficult enough in the best of times. Wish us luck.

We loaded up on supplies. Their house was indeed a veritable gold mine of supplies. The pantry had hundreds of canned goods. Their electricity had been out for three days so the freezer was full of meats that had thawed and were now in the process of rotting, which was a shame. We could have had a bar-b-que for a hundred people with the amount of brisket, hamburgers, chicken, and pork sausage that was rotting in the full size industrial freezer. There was a ton of hygiene products in the two bathrooms. We grabbed all of those as well. There were enough batteries to power a small city for a month. Maybe that is an exaggeration, but there were all types and a lot of all of them. In the end, we spent more time at Abigail's farmhouse than we intended, but by the time we left the entire cargo area of the Xterra was packed with food and supplies. We'll figure out how to get everyone back to the farmhouse later. You don't pass up this sort of thing.

It was just past midday when we pulled out of Abigail's driveway and back on to the access road. We had stopped for a hose and walked away the zombie apocalypse lottery winners. Aside from the supplies, Abigail brought out three more guns – a shotgun, rifle and the handgun she had aimed at my face, ammunition for them, and a very expensive looking composite hunting bow and arrows for it.

"Thank you for coming with us, Abby. I really think that the more people we can get together, the better off we will all be," I said, looking in the rearview mirror at her. She had washed the make-up off her face and I felt a pang of stupidity rush through me. *How could I have thought she was a zombie?* She was a normal looking girl under all that face paint.

"I just don't want to be alone anymore. I will help in any way I can. I will earn my keep, just let me stay with you guys," she said staring back at me in the mirror.

"Don't be silly, honey," Jess said, turning in her seat to look at Abigail. "Humanity is the only thing we have left to cling to right now. We need to collect it and cultivate it. We're happy to have you." I heard the smile in Jess' voice and saw it on Abigail's face. And with that, hope continued to blossom in my heart. *There really may be hope for us yet*

***

We drove along the access road for about a mile and a half and came to the neighbor just before the freeway onramp.

"Stop!" shouted Abigail, and I about jumped out of my seat. I slammed on the brakes and turned to face her. She was pointing out the window at the farmhouse. "That's Freddie and Rebecca's house. Look at the zombies trying to get in. They could be alive inside."

I looked at Jess only briefly and was happy not to see even a hint of opposition. "Sweetheart, get your bat ready." She grabbed the handle, which was propped between her knees. "Let's go get 'em slugger."

I turned the wheel all the way to the right and drove down the dirt driveway. Halfway to the house I started blaring the horn. I counted half a dozen zombies on the front porch and a couple on the right side of the house, trying to gain entry at another point. There had to be something inside they wanted. One by one, they turned from the house and started walking toward Xena as we approached. I stopped the car about a hundred yards from the house and waited. I honked the horn every once in a while until all of the zombies headed our way. When they were about a third of the way to us, I turned to Jess and said, "There are too many to just get out and brain them, don't you think? I count nine. How many do you see?"

She counted and said, "Yeah, nine. Do you have a different plan?"

"As a matter of fact I do. Is everyone ready for the newest sport sweeping the nation? Zombie Bowling has hit the great state of Texas," I said. "I really think we can get through this if we keep our heads together. Keep thinking and don't take too many chances, but we also can't lose faith in our fellow man. We have to help where we can, right? A few days ago, I said no more chivalry for me, but I can't help who I am. I'm not sure I would call this chivalry, but I feel it is the right thing. Not sure where the hell all that came from, but I had to get it out of my head. It's been bouncing around in there, nagging at me. Anyways, you guys ready? Seatbelts on? This might get bumpy."

I grabbed the wheel tight with both hands and hit the gas. I didn't floor it, for a couple reasons. I gave it enough gas to get the car up to about 25 miles per hour. If I had floored it on the dirt driveway, I would have compromised control of the vehicle. Not good when a horde of undead is bearing down on you. Also, the windshield was already cracked; I didn't want one of them flying through it and onto our lap. I just wanted to knock them all down if I could and maybe run over a couple, and then we could finish them with the bats. Amazingly, it worked. The zombies were loosely grouped all the way across the driveway, so I aimed for what looked like the densest cluster. I hit three straight on and two deflected off to either side of the car. I watched as the three directly in front of me impacted the bumper and their lower halves disappeared from view. One was immediately dragged under the car, but I watched the heads of the other two as they flew toward me and hit the hood before being dragged under the vehicle. I kept on the gas until I got right in front of the house and then slammed on the breaks. I threw it into reverse, turned around with my arm on the back of the passenger's seat and hit the gas.

I turned the wheel and aimed for two more of the zombies. I ran over two of the ones on the ground before connecting with the two I was aiming for. I saw them as they collided with the window. A large crack appeared in the window when the zombies' heads hit it. They then disappeared under the vehicle and I drove past them about thirty yards. I stopped and put it back in drive and aimed for the final two that were still standing. "I hate open frames, and I'm a sore loser," I said to no one in particular, then hit the gas. These two were not close enough to run over at once, so I aimed to hit the man on the left with the left corner of the hood. He bounced off the bumper and to the ground off to the left.

I brought the car to a halt about ten yards beyond the downed zombies and turned to Jess and asked, "You ready?" She already had one hand on her bat and the other on the door handle. I grabbed my bat and we jumped out and commenced finishing what Xena had started. The one I didn't hit was walking toward the car. One of the others had managed to get back to its feet and was shambling toward us. Jess and I started hitting the zombies in the head one by one as we got to them. If they were on the ground, an overhead swing did the trick, and the two walking got home run swings.

The gunshot made Jess and I about jump out of our skin. I know I let out a yell and turned back toward the car. Abigail came into view from around the car with her gun in her hand. She quickly caught up to us, walked right past us, pointed the gun at one of the zombies trying to stand on its mangled legs and pulled the trigger. The crack of the gun echoed too loud in the silence of the new world.

I looked at Jess and we started to double our effort to finish this out here. Who knows how long we had before other zombies came to investigate that sound. We easily put the nine zombies down. The wheels of the car took care of three and the other six were down for good in less than a minute. As soon as we dispatched them, Abigail turned and ran toward the house, yelling all the way for Freddie and Rebecca.

"Shit," I uttered. "Jessie, get in the car, let's get over there. Who knows what's inside." We both ran and jumped into the car. I threw it into gear and hit the gas a bit too hard. The car fishtailed before catching and propelling us forward. By the time I stopped in front of the porch, the front door flew open and I saw Abigail fly into someone's arms and disappear into the darkness beyond.

I looked at Jess and shrugged. She shrugged back.

I said, "I hope this isn't a mistake. We need to get out of here, quick. The gunshot was loud. I don't like it. Now any of *them* within earshot know where we are. Also, I am starting to worry about the size of our group. Let's hope these are people able to pull their own weight and not just a couple of teenage girls."

"I don't know, Abby seems to be pretty good to have around. But I know what you mean," she responded.

We got out of the car and walked up the porch steps. The door was open and we could see several shapes inside. We could also hear what sounded like teenage girl chatter. Good for Abby, but I didn't know if it would be good for us as a group. There was only one way to find out.

"Is everything ok in there, Abby?" I asked through the open doorway.

"Stephen, Jessica, come in, everything is fine. Let me introduce you to everyone," Abby's voice came from the gloom within.

We walked from the porch into the living room of the farmhouse. It was not unlike that which we had left earlier that morning. There were two couches in the main living room. All the windows in the living room were boarded up on the inside, allowing very little light in from the outside. As soon as we walked in, I heard the sound of a gun being cocked, and I raised my bat, turning toward it.

"Who are *they*?" a male voice asked from my left. As I turned, I saw a boy of perhaps seventeen pointing a handgun at me.

"Hey!" Abby shouted. "Michael put that down. They're with me. They're cool. They saved me at my place. Put it *down*!"

The boy, Michael, lowered the gun, but didn't put it away. This was my first clue that this wasn't going to go well.

"Hey guys," I decided to break the tension as best I could. "I'm Stephen and this is Jessica. Abby asked us to stop to see if we could help you. So here we are. We aren't staying long. We need to get back on the road." I looked from Michael to the other six people in the room. A woman who looked scared out of her mind. She was probably only forty-five, but looked about sixty in the gloom. There were two girls about Abby's age, obviously twins, Freddie and Rebecca, I assumed. There was also another boy about their age with his arms around one of the new girls in a very protective manner. His forehead and cheeks were covered in acne so bad that it was obvious even in the dim room.

Abby spoke up, "This is Rebecca and Freddie," she motioned to the two girls. "You've met Michael, and this is Henry with the octopus tentacles around Rebecca."

At the slight, Henry loosened his hold on Rebecca and tried to smile at me.

"And that's Freddie and Rebecca's mom Mrs. Cartwright." Then she addressed Mrs. Cartwright. "We're headed to Houston and then to a safe place. Hey, where's Mr. Cartwright?"

Mrs. Cartwright began to sob at the mention of her husband. Abby looked from the girls to their mother and to the boys.

Michael took a step to put himself between the others and me. He said, "He went out to the barn yesterday. He got bit and never came back. Any more questions? Or are you ready to go on your way now?"

"Whoa, Michael," I said lowering my bat, but my muscles remaining tense just in case. "We aren't pirates or looters or anything like that. We are just trying to help. Has anyone checked on him?"

"No dumbass! After he didn't make it, we didn't go outside. You saw how many of them were out there. And now more are going to come now that you've been firing your gun all over the place," he said as an accusatory tone boiled up in his voice.

"Ok, calm down," I started.

"Listen here you 'dumbass'," Abby said, stepping between Michael and me, puffing herself up to appear bigger than she was. She could have been a whole five two. A full foot shorter than the boy, but he sunk back toward the others anyway. "We did what we had to do. There are nine dead walkers out there. Are you going to get out of here with us, or are you staying? Cuz, yeah, you are probably right, there are going to be more of them coming."

Mrs. Cartwright spoke up between sobs, "Harold went out to the barn to get the truck and didn't come back. He's still in the barn. Is he going to turn into one of those things?"

I looked at her trying to think of the right, tactful answer, and then realized, I didn't know the answer. "I don't know ma'am. If it were a movie, I'd say yes, but I just don't know."

"Call me Peggy, please. Thank you for taking care of those things in the yard. I don't know what to do," she looked at me, pleading with her eyes for me to give her an answer. Her eyes begged me to tell her what to do.

"Peggy, it's nice to meet you. I wish the circumstances were different, but..." I didn't know what to say so the first thing that came to mind came out of my mouth, "Would you like me to check the barn for him, Peggy? I'll do that for you."

"Yes, I would really appreciate it if you..." she started, but Michael cut her off.

"You stay away from the barn. That's our only vehicle in there. You'll take it. That's why you're really here isn't it?"

Abby again spoke up, "Shut the fuck up, Michael! In case you hadn't noticed we have a car."

"We?" his eyes narrowed at her. "You're in with these bandits?"

"Mrs. Cartwright, we'll check the barn for Mr. Cartwright," Abby said.

"He wanted to take us out of here," Peggy said. "I don't know where he was going to take us. He just said 'someplace safe'."

"Ok, we'll bring the car up front and you can follow us," Abby said. "We are going to Houston and then to someplace safe."

"You aren't going out there, you bitch," Michael barked at her.

I spoke up in what I hoped was a soothing tone, "Michael, can I talk to you for a second on the porch? Just you and me? Man to man?"

He eyed me suspiciously, but started toward the door. He stopped before going out, "You first," he said before raising the gun at me again.

Jesus Christ, that was the most unnerving thing I have ever experienced. Yeah, it's even worse than the dead walking around and trying to eat me. This kid was near losing it.

"Ok, but please lower the gun. It makes me a little nervous. I'm man enough to admit that. It is going to be hard to talk as equals with that thing in my face."

"You're just going to have to deal with it aren't you, buddy," he snarled at me.

"Ok, you're obviously the boss around here. Let's talk," I said and stepped out of the door with my back to him. I half expected to get a bullet in the back of my head for my trouble, but it never came. I stepped down the first step, sat on the top and waited.

I felt him standing over me and said, "Have a seat Michael. Come on, man to man. You've got the gun."

For a second there was no movement and I thought *this was a huge mistake.* Then he took a step down and sat on the opposite side of the step.

"What do you want?" he asked with anger.

"Listen, I only want two things here. One is already accomplished. We stopped because Abby wanted to check on her friends. Done. And we took out a few of the zombies in the process. Second, I just want to get out of here. We have a car. You are obviously the boss in there. Fine. I don't want to change that. That is between you and them. I would like to help that poor woman in there. She lost her husband. You know that. If I can help her with her grief, I want to. Obviously, if you stop me, then you stop me. All I ask is you let me check the barn. If you are really worried about me taking the truck, then come with me," I said. His face went white and he shook his head once slowly. "Then are you going to let me help her?"

"You can't go in there. He got bit man. He's going to be one of them." Now he sounded more like a child instead of a macho man.

"Listen, Michael, Come with me. I'll go in first and if he's in there, I'll be the first one attacked, ok. But let me help that poor woman if I can. I kinda want to know why her husband hasn't come out. I don't know if he's become one of *them* or not. I haven't seen anyone come back after dying from a bite. Yeah it's what happens in the movies, but we aren't in a movie are we? This is one fucked up nightmare and we don't know all the rules yet. Are you coming with me?"

I thought he was going to deny me access again. He just sat there, his gaze alternating between me and the dirt between his feet. "Yeah, I'll go. But like you said, after you. To make sure you don't try anything funny."

"There we go, Michael. Now we are getting somewhere. It's us against the zombies, right? Not me against you. We have enough to worry about; we shouldn't add fighting with each other." I extended my hand to him. "Are we a team on this mission?"

"Yeah ok," he said standing up, walking to the side of the house without taking my hand. "Let's go, you first."

"Ok," I said standing up. I looked inside and saw Jess and Abby standing there about to follow me out. "You two stay put, let the men take care of this one," I said and tried to convey with my face, that they should be ready for... something.

I walked around Michael then around the side of the house. I saw that the driveway extended beyond the house and terminated at a steel building that probably housed the family vehicle and the farm equipment.

I began to walk toward it. I was trying to look everywhere at once. The driveway was lined with oak trees that looked older than the farmhouse. The ground crunched under our feet as we approached the barn. We walked on hundreds of acorns that might, if left to grow, become mighty oaks in their own right.

"Which door did he go in?" I asked as we got to the front. There were two rollup doors, one a single and one a double, and a regular door.

"This one," he said. He pointed at the door.

"Ok, you ready?" I asked, again hoping not to get a bullet in the back.

"Yeah, you go first." The fear seemed on the verge of overwhelming him.

"Ok, I'll go in. Why don't you try to open that rollup. That way you can drive out the truck." He looked at me with suspicion again. "Look, Michael, you can trust me or not. But I want to get the fuck out of here, and the quicker we get this over with the quicker we can get away from here."

"Fine," he spat.

I opened the door. Blackness greeted me. Blackness and the stench of death. "Change of plans. I'm not going in there like this. There isn't enough light, let's get this big door up." I walked over to the rollup handle. I twisted it and prayed it wasn't locked. It clicked, turned in my hand and rolled up six inches or so on its own. "Get ready, cover me if something comes out of there." I didn't wait for an answer. I just flung the door up with all my might and took two steps straight back.

The blackness within was obliterated by the early afternoon sun. There was nothing moving inside. The front end of a Chevy Tahoe faced us. And one of *them* was in the driver's seat. It was pale and snarling at me. I cautiously walked to the driver's side of the truck. It didn't follow me with its gaze. It only stared straight ahead with its snarl not moving. I heard movement behind me and shot a glance back over my shoulder. Michael was backing toward the house. I returned my gaze to the barn. There was a tractor to the right of the Tahoe, and what looked like a combine on the other side of that. Nothing moved within. Not even the zombie inside the Tahoe.

With all the caution I could muster, I moved forward to the door of the truck. I reached for the handle, pulled it up and took a step back as I pulled it open toward me. The occupant just sat there staring out the windshield.

I looked back at Michael, who was still backing away, almost to the house by then. "He's dead. He's not one of them at all, just dead."

"How do you know? It could be a trick."

I sighed and walked to the door again. I closed it enough to slip past it. I raised the bat and nudged Harold. He fell over on his side into the passenger seat face first. A set of keys jangled to the floor at his feet.

"Shit," I said to myself. "What the fuck am I doing?" I reached in, grabbed his hand and pulled gently. He didn't move, so I increased my tug little by little. When I had him upright again, I looked back toward the house. Michael had stopped backing up, but he was still closer to the house than he was to the barn. I saw people at the windows behind him. I couldn't make out their faces, but I guessed it was everyone inside watching. I turned back to the dead man sitting in the truck. "Fuck, I'm sorry about this Harold, but there is no easy way to do this." I tugged on his arm again, and he tumbled out onto the concrete at my feet. I dragged him out all the way, laying him on his back next to the truck. I immediately saw the bite on him, a chunk of flesh missing from his right forearm. His face wasn't a snarl of hunger or anger, but of pain.

Ok, so I now knew a couple more things. The bite was fatal. That I had assumed. It must also be quick, if he was only able to get into the cab and died there. Most importantly, I now knew that their bite doesn't zombify. That definitely gave me hope. That meant that there may actually be an end to this. All we had to do was stay alive long enough to outlast them. There weren't going to be any new zombies, at least not from their bites.

"Michael, get over here. He's just dead. The keys are in the truck. Do you want me to bring it out?" I asked. I thought I knew the answer and turned to see him running toward me with the gun raised. "Fuck Michael, put that thing away. You're going to kill someone."

"Get out of there. Get away from my truck. *Now!*" he yelled at me.

He didn't have to tell me twice. I started to walk toward the house. "The keys are on the floor under the steering wheel."

He shouldered me as he walked by and went into the barn. I heard him let out a little yelp when he saw Harold. Then I heard the gun go off behind me. I spun and he was standing over the dead man with the gun still pointed at the corpse's face. Or rather what was left of his face.

"Jesus Christ," I exclaimed as I started to jog to the house. I ran around the front and almost ran straight into Abby and Jess. "Let's go. That kid is seriously fucked in the head. Harold is dead. Not a zombie."

We heard the truck roar to life and the tires squealed as it shot out of the barn and turned toward us. "Shit," I uttered, "Get on the porch." We ran around the porch and up the steps to the front door.

The Tahoe braked in a cloud of dust and rocks at the side of the porch. Michael jumped out and ran up the steps and past us into the house. We watched as he ran into a hallway and heard him violently throwing up. The three of us let out sighs of relief in unison.

We stepped back into the house and Abby was the first to speak, "Mrs. Cartwright, your husband is not one of them. I'm sorry to say, he has passed though." Peggy slumped to the couch and began to sob anew. "I think we should load up your truck and get out of here quickly. Remember what I said, Stephen and Jessica have a safe place to go. We can all go there and ride this thing out together." The twins were on the couch now also sobbing and trying to console their mother.

One of the girls – I think it was Freddie - looked up and said through tears, "Why Houston? There are going to be millions of those things there. Why not just stay here?"

"Because we've made a lot of noise and more of those things are going to be coming. We are just going into the suburbs, grabbing a family – with two little kids – and getting the hell out of there," Abby said.

"We aren't going anywhere with you," Michael had reappeared. He was wiping his mouth. Thankfully, the gun was nowhere to be seen, but he was very resolute. "We aren't going with you into the city. It's too dangerous. Right Henry? Freddie? Rebecca? Peggy? Look, Stephen, I was a shit. I apologize for that. I was scared. I guess, I'm man enough to admit that too, but I am also man enough to know a suicide mission when I hear it. I'm sorry, but we are staying here."

"You idiot!" Abby shouted at him, "There is safety in numbers." He flinched at her words, but then hardened. He shook his head violently.

"Abby, maybe it's better this way. We can stop and pick them up on the way back. What do you think?" I asked her.

She turned on me. "Just leave them here? They couldn't even take care of themselves before we got here."

"They have the truck now. They can lock themselves in again and we will stop on the way back. I promise, we'll stop on the way back," I told her.

"Yeah, we'll go with you when you get back. But we shouldn't all go into the city," the cowardly Michael said.

"Fine, is that how you all feel?" she asked the rest of them. No one met her eyes. Henry was nodding, as was Rebecca. "Fine," she said, turned and walked out the door. "We'll see you in a few hours then. Try to load up the truck, if you aren't too scared to do that much."

Jess followed her out the door and the last thing I saw was a tear fall from Michael's cheek to the floor. "We'll be back for you. That is my promise." I turned and walked out after the other two.

***

We drove in silence for fifteen minutes and then the floodgates apparently opened in Abby, "What the fuck is his problem? Fucking pussy! Piece of shit! What the hell is wrong with him? We saved his ass, and he is just letting us go alone? Fucker!" she shouted out the window she had just rolled down.

Jess turned in her seat and reached for her hand. Abby gave it eagerly. "We'll get them on the way back. He's just a scared little boy who feels like he needs to protect the girls. That's all. We'll get them. He'll be calmer when we come back. Then we'll be all the stronger."

We drove in silence from there until we hit the outskirts of Houston.

The closer we got to Houston the worse the traffic accidents and vehicular carnage became. Fortunately, most of the problems were on the other side of the freeway. It seemed that most people were trying to leave the city a couple days ago. It was the same as we experienced trying to leave San Antonio. This time however we were on the inbound side of the freeway and didn't have to contend with much of that. There was the occasional smash up. Most of them appeared to be head on collisions, which we easily maneuvered around.

As the accidents increased so did our sightings of zombies. Most of them were on the other side of the freeway and appeared to be trying to get over the median in order to get at us. It was actually rather comical. We watched one zombie after another take a header over the concrete barrier into the asphalt. We chuckled a little bit. Then as the tension from the past few days started to release, the chuckles graduated into full on laughing our asses off. They weren't trying to climb over the thigh high barrier at all. They were just walking into it and their forward momentum caused them to plunge head first over and face first into the gravel-strewn center of the freeway. Most of them recovered instantly. They struggled to their feet and moved toward the vehicle. We were past them by the time they were on their feet in most cases. There were some that we watched hit the ground so hard that the contents of their skull spilled on the ground. These didn't get back up.

Once we started to get close to the city, I kept my speed well below the posted speed limit. In fact, I began to feel like a very old man for driving so slow on a fairly open freeway. I just couldn't help feeling nervous that either another car would come out of nowhere fleeing the city or a zombie would step out from one of the accidents right in front of me. I didn't want our day to end like that.

"Ok ladies," I said. "Are you ready to stretch your legs? It's time to get gas. Abby, would you reach into the back and grab the hose, please? Jessie baby, would you give her the Leatherman, please? Abby, would you cut me about a five foot piece off that hose? Let me know when you've got it and I'll stop at the next accident and see what we can get out of one of the tanks."

Two minutes later Abby said, "Got it."

"Awesome, ok here we go," I said. I pulled alongside an accident on the right. It was another head on collision and the driver of the wrong way vehicle had been thrown through the windshield into the windshield of the other car. I pulled up until I guessed that my gas tank was roughly in line with the gas tank of the eastbound Ford Focus. "What no full serve around here? Can you two cover me while I do this? No shooting anywhere near where I am, please Abby. There are going to be gas fumes all around me."

"Duh!" was her response.

"I'm just making sure. I don't feel like going boom. Ready? 1, 2, 3 here I go." I flung the door open and grabbed the hose from Abby. She got out on my side as well, walked to the back of Xena and stood there surveying the local surroundings, gun in both hands pointed at the ground. Jess got out, came around the front of Xena and stood there with her bat staring across the freeway toward the city. I moved to my gas cap, opened the cover and spun the cap off. I turned around, opened the cover on the other car's gas cover and spun the cover off it as well. I thought for a second that I had gotten lucky again, choosing a car without a locking gas cap.

I slid one end of the hose into the other car's tank, and stuck the other end of the hose up to my lips. There was a moment of nostalgia as the aroma and taste of the hose entered my system. I drank from the hose on many a hot summer day when I was a child. This was back before bottled water was the only way anyone would drink water. Then I sucked with all my might. I could feel the fact that I was getting more than air. I had never siphoned gas before, so I had no idea how long this was going to take to get going. It turns out that it doesn't take that long. I sucked until I was choking on gasoline. I coughed it out and shoved the hose into Xena's tank and held it with one hand while I gagged on the fumes and taste in my mouth.

"There's one coming. She's almost to the barrier," Jess told us in a calm voice.

Abby asked her, "Do you need help? This side is clear for now."

"No you stay over there. They have a tendency to come out of nowhere. How much longer Stephen?"

"No idea. Never done this before," I said between coughs. My head was starting to throb again. I couldn't feel if the gas was still flowing through the hose or not, so I inched the hose out until it was about a half inch out of the tank. I could see the golden stream of gasoline flowing out of the hose and into Xena's thirsty tank. I heard Jess giggle and I looked toward her.

She looked back at me and said, "She fell over like the others and smashed her face really good. Let me get her before she gets up." I watched her walk out of my sight and heard the thud of the bat against a solid object. I had heard that sound enough since we left my apartment to know she was connecting with skull. And then she was back at the front of the car. "All done. But I did see three more coming. We have about a minute or so before they get to the barrier. How is everything back there Abby?"

"Still nothing. When they get to the barrier, let me know and I'll come help you take care of them," she answered calmly.

"Wow!" I said amazed. "Am I really hearing this? We are this acclimated to this situation already that we can calmly discuss it like we're going to help each other bring the groceries in from the car?"

"Yeah," Abby said.

"Pretty much," Jess said.

I laughed and said, "Wow, this is pretty fucked up. I'm glad to have you two on my side." I went back to looking at the flow of gasoline. Or lack of flow. "Ok, looks like this one's empty. Let's get back on the road. We'll make it there and out again. We can fill back up if the opportunity arises." I yanked the hose out of both cars, tightened the cap, slammed the cover and stood up on the rail that ran the length of Xena on both sides. I reached on top and opened a compartment above the cab and threw the hose in, closed it and jumped into the driver's seat just in time to see two nude zombies – one male and one female – take a dive over the barrier. Another one was perhaps five feet away from taking that same trip. I looked to my side as Jess and Abby were slamming their door shut. "Hold on girls."

I didn't exactly hit the gas. I drove as I had been – very cautiously. I drove along and watched zombie after zombie tumble over the barrier onto our side. They at least weren't learning from their buddies' mistakes. We eventually stopped laughing at them. We saw smoke in the distance all along the skyline ahead of us. It looked as though there were half a dozen large fires burning out of control all over the city. They looked far enough from where we were headed, so I didn't worry about them too much. I did wonder how long one of those, burning out of control, would take to either burn itself out, or consume the entire city of Houston. That would be something else to discuss with Jake and Janus.

"Our exit is next," I said as we passed a sign that read "Walker Street Next Exit". "Ten minutes tops and we should be there."

Ten minutes turned out to be about thirty. Abandoned vehicles clogged the streets and we had to take two detours before we even got to Jake's neighborhood. Once we got into the neighborhood, the congestion became one of walkers, shamblors and zombies instead of cars, trucks and minivans. I kept our speed at about twenty miles per hour once we got into the neighborhood. I avoided the zombies that I could easily, but didn't swerve too much to avoid them. I deflected about twenty-five and ran at least ten down head on.

I turned down Jake's street and there were at least fifty of them on this one block. They must be able to sense food near but not exactly where it is, because they were not all crowded around Jake's house.

"I'm going to go zombie bowling up and down the street a few times in the hopes of getting Jake's attention, so he will be ready to let us in when we get to his front door. Any objections?" I asked.

"Nope," Abby said.

"Sounds like a great plan," Jess said. "Wait!" I turned toward her in time to see her mouth closing in on mine. After she kissed me she said, "Good luck, baby."

I smiled as I turned forward and accelerated to twenty miles per hour and aiming for as many zombies as I could. When I got in front of Jake's house, I blared the horn. I turned around at the end of the block and saw that there were about ten zombies trying to get up. I aimed for these on my second pass, again blaring the horn when I got in front of Jake's house. After two more passes, another fifteen or so zombies were on the ground who were not trying to get up. I had taken out about half of them, and more importantly, I had cleared the area in front of Jake's house.

I drove past the house one more time and stopped just beyond the front sidewalk leading up to his front door. I threw the car in reverse and backed up over the curb and straight up to their tiny front porch. Unlike the farmhouses, Xena actually completely blocked the porch steps.

We had to climb over the railing on the side of the porch. I was the first over. Then Abby jumped it as only a teenager could. The front door was opening and I saw Abby disappearing inside. I was standing at the side of the porch where Jess was trying to climb over the railing when I saw a tall bald zombie come up behind her and grab hold of her hair.

Jess screamed as the zombie yanked her backward out of my reach. Her bat flew from her hand. Then I saw the side of the zombie's head explode outward and fall to the ground. My eyes saw this at the same time as my ears registered the sound of a gunshot. I was already half way over the railing when the zombie's head exploded.

I grabbed Jess' hand and yanked her to her feet, bent and grabbed the bat off the grass. "Get up there, now! Go!" I screamed at her. She did as she was told.

After she was past me, I realized what had happened to the zombie that had grabbed her hair. My mind did the quick calculation and I looked where I thought the bullet had come from – the neighbor's house. I didn't see anyone. It looked like an empty house, like the majority of those in this neighborhood.

"Get the fuck inside you idiot!" the voice came from the roof next door. When my eyes pinpointed the figure on the roof, I froze. My mind could not comprehend what I was seeing.

I saw a man sitting on the gable of the front of the house. He was holding a rifle, wearing a blue sundress, white socks and combat boots. He wasn't a petite man. He was possibly six and a half feet tall. I just stood there staring. The man in the dress with the gun was yelling, "Get inside and go to the bedroom. You can gawk from there."

From behind me, I heard Jake and Jess screaming my name. It was Jess' voice that got me moving. I turned and vaulted the railing, flew inside the door and tripped over the entryway. Jake slammed the door behind me. I lay on the foyer floor surrounded by six people. Each of the six had various looks of fear, horror and amusement on their faces.

I sat up and said, "I need to thank the woman next door. Take me to your bedroom, Jake."

***

"Well, are you a fucking sight? What is this shit? Duct tape?" Jake asked me, yanking me up from the floor. "What happened to your head?" I winced as I put my weight on my legs again and the sudden movement jarred my. "And who are these lovelies? I thought you were coming with Jess, I assume that's you," he pointed at Jess, "and another couple. Intros are in order here."

I waited for my head to stop spinning. A few moments later, I looked at Jake and started making introductions. "Jake, Janus, Maggie, Little Jake, this is Jessica and Abigail. Now can we save the mix and mingle for later? I need to talk to your neighbor. She just saved our ass out there." I started for the stairs and before I got two steps, I heard Jake behind me.

"Woman? Stevie, Big Gay Mark lives next door. What are you talking about?" he called after me. Then in a quieter tone, I heard him ask, "What's up with him? He's safe now. Where is the other couple he told me about? It's nice to meet you by the way, Jessica."

Really Jake? Just breathe, Steve. Just breathe and get upstairs.

I held onto the banister all the way up to the second floor. I heard many footsteps following me. When I got to the top, I turned right, walked down the hall to Jake's room and went right in. When I got to the window, I opened the blinds and the window itself. I looked across the open space between the two houses. I could have been looking in a mirror at Jake's house. There was a window directly across the void. The blinds were closed. I waited.

"Stevie, talk to me." Jake said calmly, his enthusiasm at seeing me tempered a bit by my actions and sharp words.

I looked at him and saw that he was a bit worried. I had mixed emotions about that. On the one hand, I felt bad that our reunion wasn't what he had hoped for, but on the other hand, I think I was going to need to have him worried in order to get them all out of here. I looked him directly in the eyes and forced a smile.

"I'm sorry man. It's been a very rough past few hours. Trust me," I said and took two limping steps toward him and embraced him. I hugged him tight. "It is so fucking good to see you man." Then I lowered my voice and whispered in his ear, "We have to get the fuck out of Houston. Do you trust me?" He nodded. "Then if you have ever trusted me, trust me now. We have to go. Soon!"

A loud voice came from behind me, "And I'm the one they call 'Big Gay'?"

I turned around and went back to the window. "Mark! You big flamer! I owe you my life man."

"We need to talk, but this ain't the way," he said and inclined his head down below us. There were half a dozen zombies below us. Looking and reaching in vain up at us. "Oh, and it's good to see you again, Steve. I'll be right back with something. Pop that screen out." He produced a knife and proceeded to slice along the frame of the screen on his window. When he had three sides cut, he grabbed it, yanked it the rest of the way off and dropped it down on the zombies below. He then turned and left my view.

While he was gone, I pulled the screen out of the window frame and dropped it down to the ground below. The zombies took no notice. They just kept looking up at me and reaching toward me in what looked like a synchronized version of Luke Skywalker trying to use the force to draw me down to them. I wanted to laugh at that thought, but my mind was starting to come apart thread by thread. There were too many things going on here. And none of them were good.

After what seemed like an hour, but was really only a couple minutes, Mark came back to his window with several things in his hands. He set them down on the floor out of my sight and picked up what looked like twine and a bell. He tied a knot around the bell and leaned out the window. "Steve, catch." After I leaned out he tossed me the care package. It made a small metallic clink in the air before it was in my hands. It was a bell. "Untie it," he said to me.

I did as instructed and he pulled the twine back. He tied something else to the twine and again tossed it over to me. When I caught it I looked at it. I was holding a walkie-talkie.

"Awesome, Mark," I said across to him.

"Ok, close the window and make sure it's on channel thirteen point two. Oh wait, the bell. Tie the bell to the string and let it dangle under the windowsill. I'm doing the same on this end. A way to get each other's attention if the walkies are off." he said and slid his window mostly shut, leaving only enough space so the string could be pulled if needed. I saw him walk away and it looked like he sat on a bed or chair in front of the window.

I tied the bell to our end and closed the window in the same manner. I switched on the walkie, it powered on and the display read 13.2. Almost instantly there was a crackle and then we all heard Mark's voice come tinny through the speaker, "Big Gay Mark here. World travelers, are you there? Over." There was a short static burst.

I depressed the talk button and said, "World Travelers here, thanks Big Gay Mark. When did you decide to become a cross dresser? Over."

Static and then laughter. It was a glorious sound. I didn't know I was craving laughter until his hit me squarely in the heart. I smiled and just listened to him laughing. "Steve, I didn't intend to come out as a cross dresser today. But you folks looked like you might need a hand, and I didn't have time to change. Over."

"Mark, you can wear a tutu and football helmet for all I care. I mean it, I owe you my life. Over."

"I'll let you return the favor if the chance arises. Trust me. So tell me, what news from the outside world? I assume you came from San Anto today? What's it look like out of town? Over."

"Mark, let me gather everyone in here so I can tell everyone at once. Over." I looked around and Jake and his whole family were standing just inside the doorway. "Ok, everyone get comfortable. I don't know how long this is going to take." The six others came in and gathered around. Jess and Abby sat on either side of me, and Jake and Janus sat on the floor in front of me with the two little ones sitting quietly between them.

The kids looked so scared. I decided to keep things as general as possible for now.

When everyone was situated, I took a deep breath, depressed the talk button and placed the walkie in my lap. "Mark, can you hear me ok? Over."

"Loud and clear boss. Fire away, how bad is it? Over."

I depressed the button again and began. "I don't know how much you all know from TV or other sources, but here is the gist of what I know. Big cities are bad places to be. Even in the suburbs. I can only imagine what it is like downtown. San Antonio is in the same boat. It looks like this thing is pretty much global. Which sucks b..." I caught myself with the kids in the room, "Which sucks. I seriously doubt if there is any help coming. Which means surviving is up to us. And like I said, big cities like Houston and San Antonio are bad places to be." I looked at my watch and saw that it was already sixty thirty. "I don't think we can get out of here tonight and to safety before dark. Jess, Abby and I are leaving early in the morning. We found a place between here and San Anto that seems great. Easily defended, and just about perfect. As perfect as we can ask for under these circumstances. I obviously can't make any of you come with us. But I did come all this way to try to convince you. The concentration of *them* between here and the suburbs is bad. And if *they* weren't bad enough, it looks like Houston is burning. It looked like it was downtown, but who knows.

I counted at least four separate smoke plumes. Huge ones. And there is no one left around to fight those fires. That is about all I want to say right now. Except, Mark, you are more than welcome to join us. You are a damn good shot with that thing and I know for one that I would love a few lessons. I guess that's an over, Mark," I said and let go of the button.

"Shit, do you think the fires will get this far before morning? Over."

"No. They were pretty far off. It may take a couple days, and who knows, they may go out on their own. But I am not going to base my survival on that slim possibility. Over."

"Agreed. I will start getting my shit together. Give me a couple hours to gather it and get ready. Can we talk again later when we can be more open? Over." He apparently could tell I was holding back because of the children. And I wanted to kiss him for that (not to mention for saving Jess).

"Mark, that would be a perfect idea. How does nine o'clock sound? Over."

"Perfect. Talk to you then. Over and out." There was a final static blast and the walkie's speaker went quiet. I clicked it off.

I sat there looking down at Jake, then Janus, then each of the children. I waited. I was done giving details. Anything more would be fodder for nightmares for my godchildren, and I wasn't going to do that to them. This is scary enough without having all the details.

I looked from one child to the other. The fear on their faces broke my heart.

"Come here you two. Give me a hug." I spread my arms wide. They both stood up and jumped into my arms. Maggie kicked my shin but I barely felt it. I relished the feel of the kids in my arms.

I instantly knew coming here was the right thing to do. When they let go I was sniffling and tears were streaming down my face.

"Why are you crying, Uncle Steve?" Maggie asked.

"Because I am so happy to see you guys. I missed you so much," I told her. I couldn't tell her that I was so very scared for them. I was scared for us all.

"Can I talk to you alone for a minute Steve?" Janus asked me. "Jake can you take the kids downstairs for a minute? I have to ask Steve something really quick."

Jake looked at me and I shrugged.

"Ok. Come on kids. Let's get the last of the cookies ready for dessert," Jake said as he ushered the children from the room. When he got to the threshold, he turned and looked at me. "Now remember Stevie, no hankie-pankie for old time's sake." He actually let out a genuine guffaw as if that were the funniest thing he had ever said. That was Jake – never one to pass up a joke that may make a situation uncomfortable. And he just walked out of the room chuckling to himself.

When Jake said that, Jessica's head whipped around so fast that her blond hair looked like an umbrella opened wide. I looked at her and sighed. I rolled my eyes and shook my head, trying to convey that there was nothing to worry about. Whether it worked or not, I had to wait until later to find out.

When the others were all on their way downstairs, Janus turned to me and said, "Come here a minute Steve, I want to show you something and ask you something." She turned and left the room. She walked down the hall and into the first bedroom at the back of the house. She walked to the window and gazed into the distance. "I saw them this morning. I didn't say anything, because I didn't know what to do," she said with her back to me. She continued, "I am so scared Steve. This is our home. Everything Jake and I have worked for is in this building. I'm scared for the kids. They are everything to us. Thank you for coming. I'm so scared," she said turning from the window. There were tears streaming down her cheeks. I took one tentative step forward and stopped. She negated the gap between us and threw her arms around me in an instant. "Can you get us out of here? Can you really? You have to. You just have to!"

I hugged her back and said in her ear, "Janus, I will do everything in my power to get us all out of here. That is why I came after all. It isn't going to be easy, but I think we can come up with something." Her hair smelled musty, as if she hadn't showered in days. It wasn't a bad smell. It was very womanly. All of our old times came rushing back. The good as well as the bad. I don't understand the power of smells, but that amazed me and overwhelmed me. "What did you want to show me?" I asked

She let go of me and walked back over to the window. There was a very clear view of the distance from there. I could see smoke rising in that distance. Not four plumes, either. Now I counted six. The nearest one couldn't have been more than five miles away.

"See that close one? That one wasn't there this morning. I noticed it around lunchtime," she said pointing to exactly where I was already looking.

"Shit," I whispered. Is someone setting them on purpose?" I asked the empty room.

Janus must have thought I was asking her, because she answered me absent-mindedly, "I don't know Stephen. Get us out of here before we find out, please."

"I will, first thing in the morning. As soon as it's light out. Now all we need is a plan and a little preparation," I said turning to her. "Janus, will you listen to me? I have some pretty crazy ideas, but they all have safety and survival in mind. Will you do what needs to be done?" I asked her gravely.

She nodded, "Get my babies out at least. I'll do whatever you want if you get them out of here safely. Please…" she trailed off and began to sob.

I hugged her again. "I will," I said stroking her hair.

It took her a minute to stop the tears from flowing. When she had composed herself, we left the room and walked down the stairs together. At the bottom, she went to Jake and hugged him. She motioned to their kids and they came and formed a group hug. I walked to Jess and hugged her tight. She was a little stiff at first, but eventually softened and hugged me back. She held on to me possessively. After a few seconds, I felt two more arms wrap around us.

"You two are a bit young, but I'm going to call you mom and dad," Abby said.

Jess and I looked down at her, saw the look of sarcasm on her face and all three of us burst into laughter. It was a beautiful sound, one that I will remember for the rest of my life, however long that may be.

I spent the next hour looking through their bug-out bags. Going through their garage and adding tools to the bags, and filling the back of their Suburban (good ol' Texas and their big ol' truck fetish) with the bags and any supplies that I thought we might possibly need. In truth there wasn't as much as I had hoped we could use.

"You've gotten too comfortable my friend," I told Jake as we were loading the last of their stuff into the back of the truck. "I've got this tiny little apartment, but I had most of the things we used to talk about as kids."

"I know man. I have gotten comfortable. The American Dream has taken over my life. Thank God you never grew up, huh?" He elbowed me and laughed.

We both jumped when the sound of pawing on the metal garage door directly behind us began. "Fuck, I hate that they don't make any noise," I said. "They can sneak right up on you. We've had some close calls because of that. We need to stay on guard always, okay?"

"Yes sir, Steve-o, sir!" and he mock saluted me. This salute ended with his customary bird salute – middle finger extended toward the ceiling and the rest of the fingers curled down against his palm.

I smiled and hugged him. The sound of hands scraping behind us creeped me out, but I love this guy. We grew up together and I found a comfort in that hug that I couldn't find in anyone else.

"I found two rolls of duct tape out here. Do you have anymore? Inside, maybe?" I asked.

"I think that's it man. To be honest I didn't know we had those," he said.

"Ok, the kids get priority. If there is any left then you and Janus can have what's left…" I started.

"Janus. The kids, then Janus. I'm too quick for those things. Protect my family with your fancy armor," he said sarcastically, but his face was deathly serious.

"No worries man. We're going to get the fuck out of here and hit a hardware store and get everyone a fancy duct tape suit of armor. It *has* saved my life twice already. Of course, it is starting to smell. But that is a small price to pay if you ask me."

"I didn't. In fact I couldn't hear you over the smell," he said grinning.

"Fuck you, ass," I said, returning his smile.

"You're not getting anywhere near my ass."

"Come on let's get back inside. We need to come up with a plan, at least the beginning of one before we get Mark on the horn. We are getting the fuck out of this deathtrap at first light," I said.

"Deathtrap, sweet deathtrap," he said. "But it's my deathtrap. Come on, I want to get to know this little hottie you brought along with you."

"Hands off, fucker," I said, hitting him in the shoulder and laughing. The laughter caused a fresh round of pawing at the metal door.

We walked into the house and the seven of us sat at the table and ate a dinner that consisted of Cheerios in powdered milk. It tasted truly horrible, but no one seemed to mind. It was just nice to have a meal like a family. It was almost like normal. There was no talk of plans or zombies or escapes. The kids regaled us with what had been going on in school the week before. Jake told us about his last business lunch where he cracked a very inappropriate joke that caused the client to spit his wine across the table all over Jake's boss. Jake said that if the client hadn't doubled their contract he was sure that he would have lost his job for that one.

"I hear the bell mom," said Jacob. The room went silent and we all listened. We all heard it and it was a veritable stampede to get up the stairs. We stumbled all over each other into Jake's bedroom. It must have been pretty comical to see the seven of us come piling into the bedroom one after another, Abby and Little Jake trying to come through at the same time and crashing into the sides of the door, falling to the floor, laughing hysterically.

Jake was the first to the walkie-talkie. He flipped it on and immediately Mark's voice came through loud and clear, "Big Gay to the World Travelers and the Home Bodies. Y'all look like you're having a good time. Good for y'all. You ready to get down to business now? Over." That question broke the feeling of euphoria in the room instantly.

Jake put the walkie up to his mouth and hit the transmit button, "Mark, give us a minute to get the kids to bed," he said.

"No problem, I'll be right here waiting. Over." Mark said.

"You talk, I'll put them to bed. You can fill me in when I get back," Janus said. She ushered the kids out of the room and down the hall after pulling the door most of the way shut behind her.

"Okay Mark, we've gotten our Suburban ready for the morning. We haven't really been able to discuss plans yet, but I guess that's what we can do now, right? We brought up extra batteries. Over." Jake said into the walkie-talkie.

"Me too. I figured this was going to be a long conversation. Over." Mark's disembodied voice said out of the speaker on our walkie.

It was, indeed, a long conversation. We changed our batteries out twice. We all talked well into the night. When we were finished, we had a plan, and everyone in the room was yawning.

Mark is supposed to ring the bell at six in the morning. About a half hour before the sun rises. I just looked at the clock on my phone and if I went to bed right now, I would get seven hours sleep before getting up for the escape. But I am not going to sleep right now. Jess is giving me that "come hither now, or die" look. And I feel "up" to the task.

Good night no one.

Thursday, September 20, 2012 (handwritten)

Digging graves by hand is very hard work, especially when you have to stop occasionally to kill a zombie or two. We had to bury the dead today. Even the body of... well, I'll get to that later. There is a lot to get down before I can write about that.

Our 6am wake up bell never came. Instead of waking to the sweet tinkling of a bell, a foundation-shaking explosion wrenched us from slumber. I hadn't slept well, and when the thud-boom of the explosion went off, my eyes shot open and I sat bolt upright. I looked out the window at the full dark sky and as I watched, the darkness turned to an orange-red glow to the west. I stood up and tried to run to the window. The house rocked with the shockwave of the explosion as I got half way there and my legs seized up as they had the morning before. Not as bad, but enough to stop me dead in my tracks. Jess was up after me and she was at the window looking to the right straining to see the source.

"What is it baby? What happened?" I queried.

"I can't tell. It's out of view from here. But it was close. Look how bright it is out there. It's like daylight. This is bad, Steve." she said, still trying to see.

The pain subsided and I finished the journey to the window and stood next to Jess. I put my arm around her and tried to see. I had no better luck than she did.

Behind us, the sounds of a house awakened suddenly and violently came to my ears. I heard Maggie crying and Jacob calling for his mommy. I heard footsteps run past the door in their direction and heard Janus begin to comfort the kids. Then from our doorway came Abby's voice.

"That was close. I can see the fireball from the room I'm in."

Jess and I both turned around and saw her standing there in a pair of pajamas she'd borrowed from Janus. Her eyes were wide and worried.

"Show me," I said and strode across the room to the door with Jess right behind me.

Abby turned around, we went to the west end of the house and she pointed to the window. Jess and I walked to it and looked at a scene that could have been straight out of Hell itself. There was no fireball left, but there was a huge plume of smoke illuminated from below by flames shooting a couple hundred feet in the air.

"Shit," I whispered, "that's close. No more than a mile. Right outside the housing tract I think. Fuck, we can't wait for light now. Who knows how fast that is going to spread, or to where."

"Well, isn't this a Kodak moment?" came Jake's voice from behind us. I spun around and he had a huge grin on his face. "I guess modesty is a thing of the past?"

I laughed and looked down at myself and then at Jess. I was wearing a pair of boxers and she was wearing a thong and bra.

I touched Jess on the elbow and she jumped. She had been completely mesmerized by the flames. She slowly turned and I said to her, "Come on let's get dressed. There's a lot to do, and now I think we had better make it quick."

"Yeah," she said and walked in a daze back to our room. I followed her in and shut the door behind me.

"Baby? Are you ok?" I asked her and took her into my arms. "Hey, talk to me. What's up?"

It seemed like she was in a trance. Holding her seemed to snap her out of it. She tilted her head back and looked me in the eyes.

"I'm sorry, Stephen. I've just got a very bad feeling about today. Make love to me again before we get going. Please. I want to feel close to you again, before everything gets crazier. I'm scared. Please Stephen," she said with an earnest yearning on her face. I couldn't have denied her if I had wanted to. Which I didn't.

The lovemaking was frantic, and by the time we climaxed together, Jess was sobbing. I lay on top of her panting and hugging her. I wanted to keep complete skin contact with her as long as possible. I kissed her face repeatedly. I kissed her lips, her eyes, the tears running down the sides of her face. I only stopped when there was a soft knock on the door and Janus' voice came through the door.

"You guys ok in there? Everyone out here is ready to start. Mark wants to talk, but he wants you there, Stephen."

"Ok," I said over my shoulder. "We'll be right out." When I said that Jess' arms flew around my middle and she pulled me down again.

She put her mouth close to my ear and said with great urgency, "I love you, Stephen. I'm yours. Let's get out of here. Let's get out of here now. I want to feel this," she raised her hips up into mine, "A million more times before we die."

"Mmmmmmm," I managed at her hip movement. And then, "I love you, Jessie. We're going to get out of here, no matter what it takes. We went over everything last night. This explosion has just moved our timeframe up a little bit. It will be a little more dangerous in the dark, but it won't stay this dark for long, and with the flames, it won't even be that dark. Let's get dressed and get out of here. I can't wait to do this again tonight in our farmhouse." I kissed her deeply before sliding off her. We dressed and joined the others in Jake's bedroom.

As I expected, Jake had a big "I know what you were doing" grin on his face. Janus had a smaller, more subtle version of the same grin. At least until she saw Jess' eyes. The grin evaporated into the air as she came forward and took Jess' hand, guiding her to the bed. They sat there and Jake handed me the walkie-talkie. I couldn't tell you what Janus had seen in Jess' face. Must be a woman thing.

"You're the leader, man. We voted before you got here. It was unanimous," Jake said.

I grabbed the walkie, "Whatever," I sighed and rolled my eyes. I depressed the talk button so that Mark could hear the rest of what I had to say. "I just want to get the hell out of here in one piece like the rest of you. We are all on the same side here. As long as we stick to the plan as best we can, I think we can all get out of here safely. By noon we'll be at the farmhouse and then we can figure out what comes next. How does that sound to everyone?" I let go of the button. Everyone in the room started to nod at me, but no one spoke.

Through the walkie-talkie came Mark's voice. "Nice pep talk Steve-o. Is everything ready over there? I'm ready to roll over here. I'm man enough to admit that I am scared shitless. Over."

"What? Our cross-dressing commando is scared? Over." I said into the walkie-talkie.

Everyone in Jake's room started to giggle.

The static burst from the walkie-talkie's speaker and was followed by great guffaws of laughter and then Mark said, "Honey, I always told you that I am more woman than you'll ever have and more man than you'll ever be. Over."

That got our side of the walkie-talkies cracking up again. I depressed the talk button so that Mark could hear it. I figured that joy might lighten his heart a little before we went through with our plan. "Mark, if you don't want to go through with what we talked about last night, I can do it. I think it is a great plan, and it'll work. I did something similar to get out of San Antonio. Over."

"No, not you," Jess said, as she stood up. I just raised my hand to calm her.

I looked at her and said quietly, "He'll do it, don't worry. He *is* man enough. It's just nerves. It needs to be him saying it though. It can't be me telling him. As long as it's his decision, it will work. Trust me."

Just as I finished that sentence, the walkie crackled and, "No, I'll do it, it's just nerves, my friend. I'm scared, plain and simple. How long do y'all need to finish getting ready? Over."

I looked around the room at everyone. "Mark, the vehicles are ready to go now. I think all we need is a couple haircuts, and then we can get this show on the road. Ten minutes? Over."

"Perfect. That will be enough time for me to get Elton into the garage and ready to travel. Actually only about five minutes for that. Then I am going to start the plan. I'll let you know when I start via walkie, ok? Over."

"No, I'd feel a lot better if you waited until we were ready to roll, that way if you needed help we'd be ready. If something goes wrong. If you trip for fuck's sake..." I trailed off and released the button, already knowing what he would say before he did and knowing the wisdom of it.

"Are you done? If I trip, then I'm done either way. For this part, I am going to be on my own no matter what. It's not going to be an issue Steve. These fuckers are slow and stupid. I just have to get a couple of them to follow me and the rest will follow them like lemmings. And if I put the couple that follows me down, then we are golden and out of here lickity-split. Over"

"You're right. Give us eight minutes before you go out there. And let us know when you do. We will be as quick as possible and ready to go in about ten minutes. Wait, who's Elton? Over."

"My dog, now quit gabbing about it and get moving. Big Gay over and out." he said.

I put the walkie-talkie down and turned to the others. "Ok, ladies, you ready for a haircut?"

They all shook their heads. Jess spoke for them all, "Obviously, we'll do it, but we don't have to like it right? I experienced firsthand why we should last night. Will you still love me when I'm bald, Stephen?"

I put my arm around her and kissed her deeply, with my other hand grabbing a handful of her blond locks. "Baby, it's only hair. It'll grow back. If they pull you down by it again..." I couldn't finish that sentence. "Yeah, I'll still love you, now get to it. Ladies, do Maggie's first and send her back in here. Jake and I are going to work on suits for the kids. You ready Jake? Got the duct tape?"

"Right here boss," he said holding up the rolls we found last night. "Come here Jakey." He handed me one roll and he got down on his knees and started wrapping the silver tape around his son's pant legs.

"Remember, not too tight. He is going to need to be able to take it off later. And he is going to need room to move in it," I said to Jake.

"Yup," Jake responded.

I started with Jacob's long sleeves, wrapping at the wrists and working my way in. It was like we were creating a small, silver mummy. Before we were even half-finished, Maggie walked back into the room. She had a huge grin on her face. Her smile lit up the room. The girls had shaved her down to a short buzz cut. It wasn't really that bad. Her beautiful face was more than enough to draw your attention away from the lack of hair.

"Look at you cutie," I said. "What do you think? I think it's awesome."

"Me too," she said and giggled. I loved her so much for that. I wondered then if her mother was taking it that well. "My head feels funny. It's naked." This came out nekkid, Jake and I burst out laughing, and Maggie joined in.

"You ready to get a fancy space suit too? Hop on the bed until we're done with your brother," Jake said.

"Ok daddy," Maggie said and hopped up on the bed and sat watching us work. The whole time she was running her hands over the stubble on top of her head and giggling. "It tickles."

As we were finishing up Jacob's suit, Abigail walked into the bedroom. She wasn't quite as thrilled with her new hairdo. She came in and sat on the bed next to Maggie. She didn't say a word. Jake and I finished the suit and stood up. Jake ruffled Jacob's hair and then said, "Ok kiddo, time for you to get your hair cut too. Run in there and tell mommy that you're next."

He did exactly that. He ran from the room as best the new "suit" would allow. Somewhat straight legged, but otherwise he was moving pretty well. That made me happy. Hopefully, he won't need to move very much, but "just in case" has been my motto thus far. That motto had kept us alive thus far.

"Your turn, Maggie," I said. She hopped happily off the bed and stood in front of us. "I know your hair feels funny, honey, but I need your arms." She giggled and put her arms down at her side.

Jake and I went to work on her. We weren't that far into the job when Jacob came running back in the room. "I'm a space fighter. I'm going to zap all the zombies." He made gun gestures with his hands and started making laser sounds. That made all of us grin, even Abigail. "Daddy, Mommy's crying. She said the pile of hair on the floor was beautiful and she didn't like it. She's funny."

I ran out of tape before finishing Maggie's shirt, so I said, "Ok Jake, the rest is on you. I've covered the most important parts, but you can finish the rest right? When you're done, come get your hair done." And I left the room to get my head shaved.

I got into the bathroom and the first thing I noticed was the pile of hair on the floor. There was long blond straight hair (Jess'), long brown curly hair (Janus' and Maggie's), short brown wavy hair (Jacob's), and long straight jet-black hair (Abigail's). The next thing I noticed was Janus standing at the sink staring at her reflection in the mirror and crying. Then I saw Jess. Her head was completely bald. They had shaved hers with shaving cream and razor. I saw electric razor laying in the tub and Jake's razor full of blond locks and white shaving cream on the counter by the sink.

The electric had run out of juice before they could get hers done, so they had switched to the old-fashioned way. What a trooper she is. She was still beautiful. There would just be nothing to grab onto for a while.

Before I could say anything Maggie came running in and said, "Mark is ready. He said 'he's going to start the division now." With the message delivered, albeit somewhat imperfectly, she turned and skipped back out of sight.

"Where's the shaving cream?" I asked. But I saw it and reached for it. As I was about to take it, Janus' hand clamped down on mine.

"You are going to take care of my kids, right? You *are* their *godfather*!" she said with a coldness in her voice that was not like her at all.

"I told you I would. I'm here because of them. I'm here because of all four of you. I love you all. That's why I'm here. And I have already risked everything to get here. Now I am going to do the same to get us *all* out of here. Not just your kids. You and Jake and Abigail and Mark and Jessie. Hell, Elton too. You are all my family now. And I'm going to protect my family. That's why there is a big pile of hair on the floor. I'm not trying to make a fashion statement here with the fancy silver suits. Mark is risking his life right now for us all, too. We need to hurry!"

Her hand released mine and she pulled it back as if she had touched something scalding. Her face took on the visage of a scolded child. "Ok," she whispered and started to walk out. Then it was my turn to grab her wrist.

"Janus, hear me. I'm sorry. I didn't mean for that to be a lecture. I'm just scared and am feeling a huge responsibility here. Would you do me a favor and check to see if the fire is getting closer, please?" I tried to put on a tone of empathy. I'm not sure if I succeeded or not, but Janus tried to smile as she walked out of the bathroom.

"I'll check," I barely heard as she walked down the hall.

I looked at Jess and said, "Ok, do it. Make me beautiful." I handed her the shaving cream and razor.

She was making the first pass with the razor when Janus returned. "We better hurry. It looks like the fire is in the neighborhood. It can't be far off."

"Ok, thank you, get Jake in here and do his hair. Hopefully, we can be on our way in five minutes. Abby, would you ask her to watch out front to see what the zombies are doing? See if the distraction is working."

The sound of a gunshot broke the silent morning outside. And then there was the muffled sound of a big dog barking. It was a very deep sound. Those two sounds together made my blood run cold. I expected the gunshot sound, but not the dog barking. I don't know why that sound scared me, but it did.

Jessica had ceased shaving my head at those sounds. "Jess, please don't stop. We need to get out of here. That would be Mark taking one of the zombies out for bait. A couple more shots will come and the zombies will have something to munch on while we leave via the front doors." Janus had frozen in the hallway listening. I yelled, "Abby, come here please." It seemed she was already on her way, because no sooner had I yelled it, than she was standing in the doorway. "Abby, could you check out the front to see if Mark's diversion is working, please honey?"

"I was on my way to do that anyway. I'll be right back. Jess, I say you leave it like that," she said pointing to the hairless strip from the center of my forehead all the way to the nape of my neck. She laughed and walked down the hall toward the front of the house.

Jess finished shaving my head, and Janus did Jake's at the same time. During the five minutes that followed, Abigail shouted back to us that the dead were indeed walking to the far side of Mark's house and disappearing around the side of it. We also heard another three gunshots while our hair separated from our heads to join the rest on the bathroom floor.

As Jess was making the last pass on my hair I heard the walkie-talkie static burst and then Mark's voice came through loud and clear. "Hey guys. It's working. A little too well I think. They are trying to get into the house through the sliding door. And there are so many of them I don't think the glass will hold up that long. You ready over there? Over."

I ran for the bedroom and grabbed the walkie. I looked out the closed window across at Mark. He looked more scared than ever. "Get into the garage. We are almost ready here. Barricade the door between the garage and the house in case they get in before we get out. Hopefully, the walkie will work in there. If not remember, when you hear three short honks open the garage door and fly out fast in case there are some right in front of it. We are going to go left out of the complex. Stay behind the trucks. We'll try to keep the way clear for you and Elton. Over."

"Roger that Steve. No matter how this turns out, thank you for including me. I appreciate it. Over and Out." he said and I watched him turn from the window and disappear.

I turned around and almost ran into Jess who was standing right behind me. "Are they ready yet?"

"Yeah, they are already headed downstairs. Let's go. I can see the flames now. I don't know if we are going to be able to make it out that way." she said with deep worry on her face.

"Then we'll find another way out. Come on," I said taking her hand and walking to the stairs. I saw Abby looking out the window at the top of the stairs. "Come on Abby. Let's go. How does it look out there?" I asked as she turned from the window and started toward the stairs with us.

Her smile said a lot. "I think it's working to a degree. There were *a lot* out there. About half of them are gone now. But there is a backup on the side of Mark's house. It's like they are standing in line on Black Friday before the stores open. It's fucking creepy. Is this going to work? There is still a ton of them out there. Maybe a hundred. None are looking toward us though. That's the good side. They're all walking toward the other side of Mark's house."

"Yeah, it's going to work," I said with as much confidence as I could muster. "I want you two to go with Jake in the Suburban. If only one of us goes out the front door, we can only lose one that way." I expected an argument. What I got were two women in my face.

Jess said, "Are you kidding me? There is no fucking way you are going out there alone. You need some back up. And I am not leaving your side now until we're dead. Got that, hero?"

Abby said, "Shut the fuck up! You're an idiot if you think we are going to let you go out there alone after all you have done for us. Stupid."

How could I argue with such rock solid logic? "Ok, fine."

The walkie-talkie crackled then, "...garage...ver?"

I pressed the button on my walkie, "Say again, Mark. Over."

The static burst, then, "In... rage... eady. Over."

I guessed at what he meant and replied, "We are almost ready here. One minute. Repeat, one minute. Over."

"Rog... Ver... Out."

I peeked out the blinds next to the window and saw an encouraging sight. There were indeed a lot of them out there, but all headed toward the diversion.

"Jake," I called. He was standing by the door to the garage with Janus and the kids. "Get in the Suburban and wait for my signal. I'll give you thirty seconds before we head out this door. Go!"

"Good luck and be careful!" he said. He opened the door to the garage and the four of them disappeared.

I turned to the two women with me. "You two ready? We stick together. All three to the driver's side. You two jump in the back and I get in the front. Got it?" I asked them. "And get your seatbelts on as quick as possible. We shouldn't be out longer than ten or fifteen seconds. No problem." I held the key fob in my fingers tight enough to keep it from falling to the floor, but not tight enough to depress the button to deactivate the alarm. I kissed Abby on the forehead and then Jess deeply on the mouth. "Ready? 1… 2… 3!" then I pressed the disarm button as I flung the door open.

***

There were no zombies between the front door and the car. This was good. However, I could see three just in front of the Xterra, which was bad. Upon hearing the door open, they turned and gave us their silent snarl and began walking toward us, which was worse. Then there were the thirty or so in front of Mark's garage door, which was worst of all. It was time to move.

"Let's go!" I shouted, hoping to draw the attention of the zombies in front of Mark's garage. I ran out the door and leapt over the railing to the left of the back end of my Xterra. I was hoping the other two were right behind me. I charged at the three zombies that were now at the driver's side rear door. I brought the baseball bat down with all my force on the first zombie. It crumpled to the ground, but another one right next to it reached for me and its arm got in the way of the bat as I tried to raise it again. Its hand wrapped around my wrist before I could pull back, and it was already lowering its mouth toward my hand. I tried yanking my hand away, but only succeeded in pulling it back a couple of inches in the thing's iron grip. At the same time, I lost my grip on the bat, which fell to the ground next to Xena.

The mouth was only inches away from my hand when a handgun appeared from my left and there was a flash, a crack, and then an explosion of brains out the back of the zombie's head, which splattered the zombie behind it and the side of my car. The grip broke and I saw the thing fall on top of the bat. That was the end of that weapon for me. I reached into my waistband, pulled out my own handgun and fired from point blank range at the third zombie advancing on me. A fourth one came shambling around the front of the car at the same moment.

I reached for the rear door handle, and it didn't open. "Fuck!" I swore under my breath. *Have to double click for the other doors.* I shoved my left hand into my pocket and pulled the keys free. I fumbled with them for a moment. Abigail appeared in front of me and shot the brain out of the fourth zombie.

"There's more up there," she said calmly. "Can we go now?"

I hit the disarm button twice in succession and heard all the locks disengage. I yanked on the door handle again and this time the door opened. It only opened about a foot though, blocked by three zombie bodies. I grabbed the side of the door with both hands and yanked. Two things happened when I did this. The first was the door budged another four or five inches. The second was I pulled the trigger on the gun. The gun went off and the window on the driver's side over the cargo area exploded. On the other side, I watched a nude – at least from the chest up – female zombie with a red hole in the side of her head fall from view.

"Fuck, get in!" I shouted at Abigail. At this point the zombies that had started out in front of Mark's garage were all in front of Jake's house, a mere ten yards away from Xena. That horde didn't concern me as much as the ten or so that had shambled into range from the opposite direction. We didn't have the Xterra between them and us like the ones coming from in front of Mark's garage.

"Jessie, Abby get in now!" I yelled as loud as I could. I was competing with the sound of gunfire. I reached behind me and pulled on the handle of my door with one hand, while I also began to fire at the approaching zombies. I feared for a split second that it wouldn't open. Maybe I had re-locked it, or it was also blocked by bodies, but it opened all the way. Out of the corner of my eye, I saw Abby was squeezing into the narrow opening in the rear door. Then Jess was pulling the trigger on an empty gun, but continued as if she were still firing. *"Jessie! Now!"* I repeated at the top of my lungs. I grabbed her upper arm and pulled.

She whirled and hit me in the side of the head with her gun. Her face was a snarl and she was screaming incoherently. As the gun connected, I saw the horror dawn on her face. She wavered for a moment as my vision blurred before righting itself again. The ringing was horrible again. Damn concussion! The number of zombies behind Jess had doubled. My vision wasn't right yet.

"Jess, get in. You have to drive now," I said shoving the keys into her hand and moving to crawl into the back seat.

I felt like a drunk trying to walk a straight line at a sobriety checkpoint. Only I wasn't trying to walk a straight line I was trying to walk around a half-opened door. And drunks at least get the opportunity to fail on level ground. I tripped over a fallen zombie limb. I'm still not sure what it was – arm, leg, head – and only the door handle saved me from toppling onto the bodies. Jess was trying to help me into the back.

"God damn it woman. Get in and start the car!" I shouted at her. "I can manage." And I did somehow. I squeezed in the back door and landed with my head in Abigail's lap. I heard Jess' door close and realized mine wasn't. I tried to sit up. But the world started to go grey on me, so I just turned my head and looked up at Abigail and said, "Door."

"Shit," she said and shoved me into a sitting position. She reached across me, grabbed the door handle with both hands and yanked. "Shit!" I heard her hiss from down the grey tunnel that was becoming my consciousness. The door hadn't budged. I was looking out at approximately twenty zombies walking toward us and my door wouldn't shut.

"Shit," I said to no one in particular. From about a million miles away, I heard the sound of jingling keys.

"Shit," came the sound of Jess' voice from the same country as the keys.

Jessie? I thought. *Jessie. My Jessie!* Just as I saw the first hand on my window, I heard the car roar to life. The SUV lurched forward and the door slammed shut a mere inch from Abigail's head, which was now in my lap.

Xena struck something and slowed momentarily, before the zombie it hit became nothing but a speed bump. Jess stopped the car.

"Put your seatbelts on and hurry. We're going bowling again," Jess said and an amazing sound followed that. The sound was her laughing. It was not even the sound of "losing it" laughing. It was a genuine laugh, as if she were finding this funny.

Abigail sat up and locked her seatbelt. I did the same. As did Jess. I was looking out my window at the horde getting closer again. It was then, that I realized that it wasn't my vision that had doubled but the number of zombies. There really were twice as many. The previously distracted zombies were pouring into the front yard from around the side of Mark's house.

Jess honked the horn three times and we watched as both garage doors rolled up much faster than I expected to see. Then I saw Jake running to get into his suburban and Mark jump onto his motorcycle. Mark was in full leathers and helmet. I imagined him in a little hat instead of the helmet and laughed along with Jess at the spitting image to the biker from The Village People.

Jess floored the accelerator and Xena and her occupants shot forward, the tires spraying grass and dirt behind it. Jess pulled the wheel hard to the right, cut across the lawn and began plowing through zombies. We bounced when we hit the concrete of Jake's driveway and shot off the other side toward Mark's driveway. Between the two driveways she again pulled the wheel to the left and shot onto the driveway aiming almost straight for the street. The rear end fishtailed and this maneuver managed to knock three more zombies off Mark's driveway. She completed the maneuvering by making yet another left onto the street.

I honestly have no idea how she kept control of the car through all of this. Of course, my head was pounding and ringing at that point. As I watched out my window and behind us, I saw Mark's motorcycle, complete with what appeared to be a very large dog sitting in the egg-shaped sidecar riding next to him, come flying out of his garage. Simultaneously, Jake's Suburban also shot from his garage. The sound of squealing tires was loud in the air.

The suburban barreled through the zombies left in Jake's driveway like the bow of a boat cutting through water. Mark, on the other hand, rode straight down the middle of the wake that Xena had cut through the horde for him, taking up his place right behind Jake.

The three vehicles raced west toward the nearest exit to the neighborhood. We didn't get two blocks. The exit to the housing tract was blocked. There was a wreckage of four vehicles blocking the main road out. I saw another two hundred or so zombies picking through the wreckage, eating victims of the accident. This must have just happened, because some of those victims were still moving.

Jess stopped, rolled down her window and motioned for Jake to pull up. As he pulled up alongside us, the zombies began to take notice, and those that hadn't found something to munch on began to walk toward us. They were backlit by the fire. It seemed the entire housing tract was ablaze. It looked like the accident happened when these poor fuckers were trying to flee the fire.

Jake pulled up alongside and Janus already had her window down.

"Can't go that way. Get us out of here. I'll follow you," she urgently said across to Jake.

Jake didn't say a word. He just hit the gas and shot out ahead of us. He snaked us through the neighborhood. Eventually we came out on the same road we would have if we had been able to leave via the main exit, just a little to the north, but safe and sound. All three vehicles were more or less intact.

***

We drove south toward I-10 as quickly as we could. When we got to the exit we had intended to take from the housing tract we saw the source of the explosion and fire. Where once a Valero gas station had been there was only a thirty foot charred crater. As we passed the crater, another explosion rocked us. This one was far off and directly behind us. Whoever was doing this was having a field day this morning. We drove on until we hit I-10. We avoided zombies when we could and slowed to deflect them to the side when we couldn't.

Mark really seemed to be enjoying this. He was the least protected of us all and must have been steering with his gun in hand, because anytime one of them got close to him, he aimed and shot it in the head. Even at twenty-five miles per hour he had undead aim. It really was quite impressive to watch after my head cleared.

When we got to I-10, we didn't bother trying to get on the westbound side of the freeway. Instead, we drove onto the eastbound side heading west. We then had to contend with all the zombies that had fallen over the barrier on our way into town. They were up and walking again. There were hundreds of them. We had to go slow and try to keep as many of them away from Mark as possible. He was going to run out of ammunition soon otherwise. And then what would he do to keep them away from him and Elton.

It took us an hour to get ten miles. Jake drove point. He created a wake that we followed. Abigail and I were shooting from our windows and taking out zombies on both sides that looked like they may get close to Mark as we passed.

This worked extremely well. When we got to the very outskirts of the city it was time to fill up our gas tanks. This went smoothly with so many of us to stand guard while we filled the three tanks at three different accidents.

After refueling, we took the duty of lead car since we were the only ones that knew where we were going. Our first stop was the

Cartwright farm. We exited the freeway as the sun was clearing the eastern horizon.

I stopped Xena, got out and stood staring at the eastern sky as the darkness evaporated into the blue of a glorious, cloudless Texas morning. Jess got out, came around the car and put an arm around my waste. She leaned her head on my shoulder and watched the world transform from a scary dark place into a bright hopeful new day. We saw no zombies anywhere. There were only the eight of us – nine if you count Elton, who was even out of his sidecar inspecting the bushes on the side of the road – marveling at the sunrise.

When we had all refilled our souls with hope, we got back in our vehicles and drove down the access road until we turned into the Cartwright driveway. The first thing I noticed was that the Tahoe wasn't parked by the side of the house. In fact, it was nowhere in sight. The second thing I noticed was the zombie on the porch. Hunched over something and eating heartily.

The zombie took no notice of us as we drove up. We parked only ten feet from the porch and still the thing didn't look up from its meal. I got out and walked right up to it. As I pointed the gun at its temple, it turned its head, silently snarled and then its face imploded as I pulled the trigger from a foot away. I looked down at the mess. I expected to see a little zombie on zombie cannibalism, but Peggy Cartwright was staring up at the porch ceiling. There was a bullet hole in her forehead. I looked around before walking back to the cars where Jake, Mark, Jess and Abigail had gathered.

"Come on, guys, let's get back to our farmhouse. We're only a couple hours away," I said to the group.

"What happened?" Abigail asked.

"I can't tell for sure," I said. "That's Mrs. Cartwright. She's been shot in the forehead. I can't tell if it happened before or after the zombie started eating her. Maybe she was bit and Michael shot her to keep her from turning. He did it to Mr. Cartwright, even though we had just discovered that bites don't cause you to turn into one of them. He was pretty scared. She may have even killed herself because of grief. I just don't know." I shrugged. "Come on, let's get on the road."

I had a very bad feeling about this situation. And I wanted to put as many miles between us and this place as quickly as possible. Little did I know that the Cartwright farmhouse wasn't the location should worry me.

***

The drive between the Cartwrights' and our farmhouses was uneventful and we made very good time.

We turned off I-10 and headed north again. We didn't encounter a single zombie between the freeway and the farmhouse. From a distance, we saw the Tahoe in the driveway. It was parked next to the pickup right in front of the porch.

"What the hell? How did they find this place?" I asked rhetorically.

"Oh my God! That would be my fault," Jess said. "I told them when you were in the barn with Michael. I was trying to explain why they should come with us."

"Ok, maybe they just took it upon themselves to find it on their own, in case we didn't make it out of Houston," I said. I was trying to convince myself in spite of the dark feeling that had taken hold of my heart.

"And Mrs. Cartwright?" Abigail asked

"I don't know, let's be careful," I said.

When I got to the mouth of the driveway, I stopped and got out. Jake and Mark pulled up next to me and stopped.

"You guys stay here. I'll signal you if it's ok to come on up," I said to Jake and Mark. I have a bad feeling about this. I'm going to try to get the girls out of my car too. They probably won't have any of that, but I need to try."

"You're the boss," Jake said.

"I'll have you covered man. No worries," Mark said as he pulled his rifle from the sidecar next to Elton the Rottweiler.

"Thanks guys," I said. I walked back to my car and got back in the driver's seat.

"Ok ladies, it's time for you to hop out and into Jake's car while I check out our home," I said. They both just looked at me with consternation. "Fine, but you are both going to get on the floor and get as low and out of sight - and line of fire – as possible. Understand? I'm going to do the same to the best of my ability. Deal?" I asked in a tone that I hope conveyed that they had better agree or get out.

"Yeah," Abigail said.

"Fine," Jess said.

"Ok, wait until I get in the driveway, and then get on the floor as low as you can,' I said driving past the driveway and then putting the car in reverse and started backing into the driveway.

They both did as I instructed, and lucky for them that they had. I only got halfway down the driveway when the first bullet came through the rear window and blew out the stereo in the center console. Plastic flew everywhere.

"You asshole," I said under my breath. I reached down, shifted into drive and hit the gas. A plume of dust shot up between the house and us. As I high-tailed it out of the driveway, I saw a muzzle flash from behind the motorcycle. Mark stood up and got back on his bike, then he and Jake were following me north on the farm road.

We drove two miles up the road. We were just far enough to be out of sight of the farmhouse. We stopped and everyone but the kids got out and began the discussions.

***

Mark began, "How many of them are there? Because I know I got one of them."

I said, "Well, that we know of, there is Paul and Tammy. Freddie and Rebecca. Michael and that other boy. So six? I'd be willing to bet that Paul and Tammy are not going along with this."

"Freddie and Rebecca aren't doing this," Abby said. "It's Michael. I doubt if Henry would be in on it either, unless he is afraid of Michael. Mark, if you got Michael, then this is probably already over. Henry won't continue without Michael."

"Ok, so you are saying that we are probably dealing with two kids here? And probably only one now?" Mark asked.

"Probably," I said.

"Ok, let's not fuck around here," he said. We don't need an elaborate plan against one punk kid. Is he likely to take hostages?"

Abigail answered, "I don't think so. But then again, I didn't think he would shoot at us either. Crazy times, unpredictable people."

"Steve, you are going to take your Xterra off-roading a bit," he said and laid out his plans for us.

***

Janus, Jake and the kids were in the lead car of the attack and were mostly going to be in front to get Michael's attention in the house. Then came Jess, Abigail and myself in Xena. Bringing up the rear would be Big Gay Mark and Elton. Everyone was strapped in tight – even the dog. This was going to be quite a bumpy ride for all of us.

Janus drove that Suburban like a bat out of hell. The engine roared especially loud when they were in front of the house. After she had passed the farmhouse, she slowed and turned off road to the right in a wide arc. We were following about ten seconds behind the Suburban. We sped toward the farmhouse, but before we got to it on the road, I pulled Xena to the right and angled toward the rear corner of the house. Ten seconds behind us, Mark and Elton rode straight to the driveway and Mark pulled a maneuver that I never would have thought possible for a motorcycle with a sidecar. He braked and jerked the handles hard to the right. He wound up facing the way we had come. He jumped off and knelt down behind the bike. He pulled his gun out. The next time I saw Mark, Janus and Jake were carrying his corpse to the front of the house.

After I saw Mark's maneuver, I saw the white Suburban disappear on the other side of the house heading for the other rear of the building. I stopped my car near the back of the building, jumped out and ran to the end of the house. I peered around the corner and saw five zombies trying to get in the back door of the place. They had heard my car as well as the Suburban, which drew their attention away from the back door. Three began to walk toward me and the other two toward the other end of the house.

Meanwhile, I heard two gunshots explode from the front of the house and a high-pitched scream from inside toward the front of the house. *Oh shit, he shot one of the girls.* I thought. I motioned to the girls that there were zombies behind the house and began to run toward the front of the house.

Then I heard two more screams. One from the front of the house that sounded like Janus screaming Mark's name in anguish and the other from directly behind me that was Jess screaming my name to alert me that she needed help.

I froze for a split second, my brain processing the different types of screams. A moment later, I was running back toward the rear of the house. When I got there and turned the corner, I saw five zombies were all crowded around someone and in the process of bringing whoever it was down to the ground. The victim was screaming in fear and pain. Jess and Abigail were firing their guns into the backs of the zombies closest to them. Only one of them managed to get a headshot.

Not knowing what was going on but trusting in my two partners, I rushed forward and joined them in trying to take down the zombies. But I was having no better luck than they were.

The zombies were not the least bit distracted by the bullets hitting them from behind. They were intent on their prey. The three of us stopped firing from the side of the building and walked right up behind the four left and put bullets in the back of the heads of each. The screams continued along with the thrashing of the victim from underneath the five dead zombies. We yanked them off to reveal Michael screaming and bleeding from at least a half dozen different wounds.

"Help me," he whimpered up at us. "It hurts so bad. It's like fire. I can feel it running through my body. It hurts." He let out one last scream of pain. His back arched off the ground and he gasped for breath. Then he fell to the dirt, and that was that.

I turned to the girls and said, "The front. I think Mark needs help." Jess and I ran around the house, but we paused a moment when we heard a gunshot from behind the house. I noticed Abigail hadn't come with us. Mark was already gone by the time we got there. Janus and Jake were carrying him up the driveway, Elton whimpering behind them.

They laid him down on the porch that had seen so much death just the morning before.

Jake said, "He said he shot one of them in the shoulder before he was shot."

"We took care of him out back. Well, actually the zombies did. We took care of the zombies though."

The front door opened and Freddie, Rebecca and Tammy came out. We all pointed our guns toward them and they all cringed back. We lowered the guns.

The girls related to us how Michael had snapped this morning and decided that they were going to come to our farmhouse and wait for us. When he was outnumbered in votes, he shot Mrs. Cartwright in the face. The other kids had followed along after that out of fear.

When they got here, Tammy and Paul had come out to greet them. Michael just shot Paul in the face, and put his body in the shed behind the house. We arrived only about an hour after that. An hour sooner and... Well, I will always wonder how many lives might have been spared if we had been an hour sooner. Mark had indeed shot Henry when we first arrived. He had hit him in the neck, and he had bled out while we were deciding how best to return. Henry had been standing at the window upstairs. According to Rebecca, he wasn't shooting at us. He was holding a rifle, but he wasn't aiming it.

The first thing we did was take the zombie corpses out of the yard and drop them with the pile we had started the day before. After that, we took Michael, Henry, Paul and Big Gay Mark around to the rear of the house and began digging the four graves. All the gunfire had attracted zombies from every direction. Like I already said, digging graves is mighty difficult work when you have to stop and brain a zombie with a baseball bat every half hour or so – we decided, no more firearms unless absolutely necessary.

We didn't get down the customary six feet, but we eventually had four holes in the ground roughly four feet deep by six feet long and three or so wide. I jumped down into the first hole and Jake lowered Michael's body down to me head and shoulders first. I laid him down and Jake helped me out. Then he jumped into the next hole and I lowered Henry down to him. Then Jake and I both jumped into the third hole and Jess and Abigail carefully lowered Mark down to us.

Finally, Tammy and I jumped down into the last hole and received Paul's body. We laid him down gently, and as we were standing up Tammy grabbed my handgun out of my waistband. Before I realized what was going on, she stuck the barrel into her mouth and pulled the trigger. The back of her head exploded up and out of the grave as the rest of Tammy fell on top of her dead husband. All the while, I just stood there in disbelief, my eyes and mouth wide open, watching the scene play out before me.

I took the gun from her hand and handed it up to Jess. I arranged Tammy and Paul so that they would be forever hugging before climbing out of the hole.

It took us another hour just to fill in the holes. It was mid-afternoon by this time and getting damn hot. We stopped for a water break. That was a couple hours ago, though. I don't think we'll be doing much of anything for the rest of the day, other than maybe killing a zombie or two. Tomorrow we are going make grave markers.

Saturday, September 22, 2012 (handwritten)

2AM

It may have been a mistake to come here. The similarities to "Night of the Living Dead" are too many. We spent most of today killing zombies. I wonder if we are still too close to San Antonio? We kept the gunfire to a minimum, yet still they came. They came from the north and the south. Some even made their way across the fields to the east and west. We have plenty of food to last us. Our ammunition is only going to last another three or four days at the current rate. We used about a quarter of it this morning to take care of the twenty that had surrounded the farmhouse. They were at every doorway and we had to shoot our way outside before we could dispatch the rest from around the house with our baseball bats. The gunfire must be drawing them in. Our group is strong, and our spirits are still high – at least on the outside.

I just talked to Jake. He is worried.

"Man, I thought this place was safe," he said.

"Jake, remember how many were outside your house. This is still nothing compared to that," I replied.

"Yeah, but you said we'd be out of harm's way here."

"I never said that. I just said we'd be safer than in the big city."

"We didn't get a break from them at all today. We must have killed a hundred of them," he said. His voice rose in pitch with each word.

"Calm down, Jake. We are going to be fine. Maybe we need to get farther out into the boonies. I thought this place would be ideal. I think we need to give it a day or two more to really see what's going to happen. Remember, we drove through from the north two days ago and from the south just yesterday. Tomorrow will be better. You'll see."

"I hope so, man. I've got a wife and kids to worry about, remember. If tomorrow isn't better, then I say we hit the road. Texas is a big place, with lots of wide-open space. We've got to find a place that is safer than this," he said. The fear in his eyes pleaded with me to help him make sense of this world.

"Jake, if tomorrow isn't better, we will try to find a better place. Go get some sleep. I'll take the first watch tonight."

"Do you promise, Steve?" he asked. "Can we really try to find a better place if this one isn't safe?"

"Dude, do you think I want to spend the rest of our lives like this? Of course, if this place isn't safe, we're out of here. Let's see what tomorrow brings. We did fine today. We have a great group here. Now go, get some sleep and be ready for your watch at two," I said, pushing him toward the stairs.

My watch was easy. Our power had gone out around noon, so I didn't have anything to see outside except the light of the moon. The house was quiet. There were no sounds outside except for some sort of chirping bugs.

Jess joined me on my watch at about ten o'clock, an hour after Jake had gone to bed. She came down the stairs as quietly as she could, but in a silent world, every footstep is as discernible as a gunshot in the distance. There will be no sneaking up on someone for a long time to come.

"Hey beautiful," I whispered as she got to the bottom of the stairs. "You don't have to stay up."

"I know that, silly. I just want to be with you," she said and gave me that smile that allowed no argument.

I smiled back at her. "All's quiet out there. I've got about four more hours until I wake Jake up to watch."

She didn't say a word. She walked up to me, grabbed the sides of my face and kissed me deeply. I closed my eyes and lost myself in the kiss for a moment. The kiss moved from standing beside the window next to the door to the couch. The kiss became increasingly passionate and Jess and I made love in the silent living room. Our desire took over, even if we were unable to fully vocalize our pleasure. The need to be as quiet as possible heightened our pleasure. Our passion climaxed with us panting into each other's necks.

As we regained our normal breathing, we heard the first troublesome sound of the night. I looked up from my love and turned my head to angle my ears toward the rear of the house. There was a thudding sound coming from the back door. Then the doorknob rattled. I looked down at Jess with concern. I was met by the blue eyes and was instantly calmed. I lowered my mouth to hers and kissed her one more time before rising and getting my clothes back on.

While we dressed, I listened to the sounds of something trying to get into the back of the house. I walked through the kitchen to the back door and watched as the doorknob twisted violently. I moved the blinds in the door an inch and looked out. An emaciated face stared down at the doorknob, as if trying to figure out how it worked. I peered around the woman and saw no other zombies.

I turned to Jess and whispered, "What do you think? There is only one out there. Should we take care of her now or just leave her until morning?"

"Are you sure there is just one?" she asked.

"The moon is full, and I can't see any more out there. If we can take care of her now, we won't have to listen to this rattling all night long. And I want to keep this place as safe as we can. I think we should take her out now and be done with her."

"Then let's do it. Do you think it's safe to go out the front door and come around the back to get her from behind?" she asked.

"It's definitely better than opening this door. We may be able to do it without making much noise. If we open this door, she'll be drawn inside. That's the last thing we want."

We went out the front door and walked around the house, using the light of the moon to keep an eye all around us as we circumnavigated the house. When we got to the rear of the house, the zombie heard us and started toward us.

"I'll walk around her and if she comes toward me, you hit her from behind," I said to Jess.

"Same plan as always. It's worked perfectly so far," she said back.

I walked out from the house and around the approaching zombie. At first it followed me, then it saw Jess moving straight toward it and shambled toward her. I completed my arc around it and moved in with my baseball bat raised. I brought it down with a grunt onto its head. It stumbled and almost fell. I pulled my bat back just in time for Jess to slam her bat down on its head. It fell to the ground and didn't move.

"Let's get back inside," I said. We walked back around the house to the front door.

We closed the door behind us and continued our watch.

I woke Jake up at two and now Jess and I are in our bed while he makes sure nothing gets inside downstairs.

Saturday, September 22, 2012 (handwritten)

5pm

Today was rough.

When Jake woke us up at eight the house was surrounded. He said he fell asleep and when he woke up, they were all around the house. There was more than yesterday morning. Thirty or so. We got everyone up and got ready to clear the perimeter of the house.

There were about ten at the front door, five or so at the back door and the rest were trying to get in through the windows all around the house. Abby, Freddie and Rebecca waited at the front door for my signal. Each of them had handguns and was ready to fling the door open and take down the zombies there as soon as they turned to come after Jake, Jess and I.

I saw that baseball bats were not going to cut it this time and got my handgun ready while Jess and Jake prepared themselves with their bats at the back door. I unlocked the door and flung it open. The zombies pressing on it fell inward toward me and I lowered my gun, quickly aimed and shot the first three in the head from no more than a few feet away. The other two moved to step into the kitchen and I quickly put bullets into their faces as well.

The way out the door was clear and I jumped over the bodies of the fallen zombies before more could take their place. Jess and Jake followed right behind me. There were zombies to the left and to the right of the door. I pointed to the left. Jake and Jess both went that way with their bats as I fired on the four that had given up on the windows and were walking toward us to the right of the door.

I turned around in time to see Jess and Jake pulverizing the two zombies over on their side with their bats. When the rear of the building was clear, we made our way around the right side of the building. We were greeted by a half dozen more of those things. They were already walking toward the back of the farmhouse.

"Fuck," I said. "Cover me." I walked toward the silently snarling zombies with my gun raised. I waited until I was within a few feet of each one before pulling the trigger. When the last one fell to the ground, we heard gunfire from the front of the farmhouse.

The three of us ran along the house to the front. When we rounded the corner, Abby and Rebecca were putting bullets in the backs of zombies' heads. The zombies had started toward the sound of our gunfire, and as soon as they moved away from the front door, the girls had flung open the door and started firing. Perfect.

Almost.

"You three stay here and keep an eye on the front. We're going to go around the other side of the house and in the back door to make sure the perimeter is clear," I said to Abby and the twins.

"You got it," Abby responded.

There were no more around the side of the house or at the rear of the house. Jake, Jess and I went into the back door, shut and locked it when we completed our circuit of the house. We walked through the kitchen to the living room and Jess screamed.

"Abby, look out!"

I looked through the living room to the front door and saw a zombie walking through the door toward the three girls on the outside. It must have walked in the open back door and through the house. Abby turned and saw the thing just in time. She ducked and lunged to the side of the doorway just in time to avoid its arms and gaping mouth. Jake, Jess and I raised our guns and fired at the zombie in the doorway. All three of us hit it. The thing spun around from the impact of the bullets, crashed into Freddie, and they both fell to the porch, with the zombie on top of the girl.

The three of us ran to the girls and pulled the zombie off her. There wasn't much blood from its wounds, but there was a little bit from the hole in the back of its head. I don't know which of us got lucky with that shot. There was also a bullet hole in the zombie's lower back as well as one in its upper back.

As soon as we got the zombie off Freddy, she began making gagging sounds and clutched at her throat. Her eyes bulged out of their sockets. They looked like they were about to explode. There was a tiny bit of blood on her cheek and at the corner of her mouth.

Within seconds she was dead.

Rebecca immediately began CPR on her sister. She was on her knees using stiff-armed compressions on her sister's chest within a second of Freddie's final breath. After three compressions, she bent further and blew deeply into Freddie's open mouth.

I watched this in a fog. I was looking for a gunshot wound on the dead girl. I thought a bullet must have gone through the zombie and into Freddie. Then my eyes focused on the blood on her cheek. The blood at the corner of her mouth had been smeared by Rebecca's mouth. Just as my brain made the connection between the blood and the girl's death, Rebecca was finishing her second set of compressions and starting to bend to blow into her sister's mouth again. I lunged, grabbed her by the back of the shirt and yanked. I also had a handful of hair mixed in with the cotton. I wasn't gentle, and pulled her completely off of her knees and onto her back next to the wall by the front door.

She stared at me with shock. She swallowed to lubricate her throat and said, "What the fuck is wrong with you? We need to try to…" she began, then grasped her throat and started to gag just as her sister had. Seconds later she was dead. The four of us could do nothing. We stared in utter helplessness as she died just like Freddie.

"What the fuck?" Abby asked.

"Yeah, what the fuck is this?" Jake echoed.

I sighed and pointed to the blood on Freddie's cheek, "Their blood is poisonous. I had no idea it was this fast acting, though."

"So they're going to come back as two of those things?" Jake asked.

"I don't think so. I don't think this is like the movies. I think they just kill. I don't think they create more," I said. "Let's take them out back and bury them with the others. We need a plan. We need to prepare. We're down to seven now.

We buried the twins in the back with the others and then came inside for rest and planning. We were in the middle of debating what to do next – stay put, head north, or head to the coast and look for an island – when Little Jake spoke up.

"Daddy, there's more of them coming up the driveway," he said with his back to us as he stared out the front window.

"Immediate business first. Let's take care of these unwelcome guests and then finish this conversation," I said.

"Jakie, come over here," Janus said to the boy at the window. When he got to her, she wrapped her arms around both of the children and hunkered down into the sofa with them.

She wasn't going to be any help.

I walked to the window and looked out. In the light of evening, I could see about twenty zombies coming up the long dirt driveway.

"This is our home for right now, guys. Let's protect it," I said. I waited for confirmations from Jake, Jess and Abby. In response, they grabbed their guns and we all stood at the front door. I reached for the handle, took a deep breath, looked each of the others in the eye and said, "Okay, here we go." I flung open the door and we stepped outside into the Texas afternoon. I was shocked to see the twins, Freddie and Rebecca, at the front of the group of zombies headed up the driveway. Their clothes were dirty and soil dropped off them as they shambled with the group behind them. They saw us emerge from the front door and snarled silently, continuing to shamble toward us in unison.

The four of us readied ourselves for the incoming wave of zombies. This was our farmhouse.

For today at least.

To be continued...

ABOUT THE AUTHOR

M. A. Rogers lives in San Antonio, Texas with his wife and three children. He is a mild mannered accountant by day, bartender on the weekend and his darker side comes out in his writing when he has the opportunity.

Feel free to connect with him at any of the following online venues:

Email: marogers@marogers.me

Twitter: http://twitter.com/myltldmn

Facebook Fan Page: www.facebook.com/MARogersWrites

Website: www.marogers.me

ABOUT THE COVER ARTIST

Website: http://cathymillerburgoyne.weebly.com

Made in the USA
Lexington, KY
23 July 2013